THE DEAD

The Dead

by

Paul Kane

Black Shuck Books
www.BlackShuckBooks.co.uk

All stories © Paul Kane, 2019

Cover design & internal layout © WHITEspace 2019

The right of Paul Kane to be identified as the author of this work has been asserted by him in accordance with the Copyright, Designs & Patents Act 1988.
All rights reserved. This book is sold subject to the condition that it shall not be reproduced in whole or in part, in any form or by any means, electronic or mechanical, including photocopying, recording, or by any information storage and retrieval system now known of hereafter invented, without written permission from the publisher and without a similar condition, including this condition, being imposed on the subsequent purchaser.

First published in the UK by Black Shuck Books, 2019

978-1-913038-02-1

7
Dead Time

45
Dead Reckoning

125
Dead End

Dead Time

It was exactly how they'd said it would be in the movies... almost.

They got a few things wrong; not many, granted, but some. The way they walk, for example. They don't shuffle or lumber along as if they're wading through tar, oh no. They move normally, just like any regular person. And they got the range wrong too. In the movies they all pretty much look the same, right? Like they need a good night's sleep or something, black bags under their eyes, maybe a few wounds here and there, broken or disjointed limbs – and yes, there *are* some like that. Okay, more than some. But there are others too, I guess the most recent, that don't look that different to the living; apart from when they open their mouths and let out those moans, of course. Then there are the ones that are virtually skeletal – see, didn't warn you about those, did they, the film guys? I mean, I never saw one that was pretty much a skeleton, but when you think about it how else are you going to look when you've been in the ground for a hundred years, maybe longer? Flesh decays, it rots – just like the whole world, eventually.

I'm getting ahead of myself, though. My name is Helen Kirby, and this is my story. You'll probably have heard dozens similar to it by now, only mine's slightly different, as you'll see if you stick with it right to the bitter end...

The first thing I can remember that New Year's morning – all right, afternoon technically – was the light streaming in through the window of my flat. Normally I would have pulled the blinds before going to bed, but I hadn't this time; probably because I hadn't *made* it to bed. And when I opened my eyes, lifting up my head, I understood why. *God, that must have been one hell of a bender last night*, I thought. My head was pounding and my mouth felt as if someone had emptied the entire contents of an ashtray into it, stubs and all. I'd been trying to quit in the run up to Christmas (those things will kill ya!) but the weed had obviously been calling to me the night before, and in my weakened condition I'd answered "Here I am, now where are my matches?"

My head was pounding, sharp pains in my temples like someone was drilling into them, and alarm bells rang in my ears. In fact my whole body ached and I felt sick to the stomach. My own fault, of course, totally self-inflicted – though most of it, I had to say, was a blur.

I managed to prise myself up off the couch where I'd collapsed, knocking over an empty bottle on the floor, and I hobbled across to the window with the intention of shutting out all that sunlight. I banged into the table on my way and several stacked exercise books fell onto the floor. Oh, that's right, I forgot to tell you: I'm a teacher in a secondary school a few miles away, year sevens. Or at least I was... before all this. Teachers are a thing of the past these days, unless you count teaching people how to survive.

I couldn't be bothered to pick the marking up; for one thing I didn't think I would have made it down there without emptying the contents of my stomach, so just got on with the task at hand.

New Year or no New Year, it was far too bloody bright for me. My eyes were slits and I had one hand up to shield them; it felt like the sun was out to burn away my retinas. The other hand was on the string that would pull down the blinds when, out of sheer habit or just curiosity, I looked out over the town that I'd lived in for the best part of seven years – ever since passing my teacher training exams.

At first I didn't think much of the fact there was nobody about. It was New Year's Day, right? People all over the town, all over the country, were having a lie in today, nursing hangovers and regretting things that they'd done the night before. I really shouldn't be surprised if the streets weren't teeming with folk.

But there was something about the quietness, something creepy I couldn't put my finger on. Not a soul about, not one person. Shrugging, I was about to pull down the blinds when I did see something out of the corner of my eye – a figure. A running figure. It was a young kid about seventeen, eighteen, in jeans and a hooded jacket. I recognised him; in fact, I think I'd even taught him at some point, but my head was too fuzzy to remember his name. No great shakes, probably trying to get back home before his parents sent out the search parties.

No, that wasn't it at all. He kept looking over his shoulder as he sprinted. He wasn't running to get to somewhere, he was running *away* from something. Then I saw what, as a gang of a dozen people emerged out of nowhere. They were running too, clearly after him. A gang thing? No, some of the people were older than him – much older, men *and* women – and they were dirty looking, you know what I mean? Still didn't connect with me at that time, I thought he'd done something like throw a stone at someone's window or something, been caught trying to break into a car...

I followed this bizarre scene for a few seconds, and as my eyes adjusted and trailed him up the road I began to notice how different the town was now. Cars were parked oddly, some fully across the road, their doors left open, abandoned. And talk about broken windows, you could have taken your pick – shop fronts, the nearby pub and bank – although I don't think the boy had anything to do with that. New Year revellers who got carried away? I'd never known it get that bad; litter in the streets, sure, but not smashed up stores. It was like a riot had taken place while I was sleeping. I guess I don't have to draw you a picture – like I said, they prepared us for it in movies long before the real thing.

The youth might have stood a chance of escape if he hadn't tripped up on the pavement. He got back to his feet again, but not fast enough. The gang were on him. My hand went from my eyes to my mouth as I watched. I was expecting them to drag him to his feet and give him a talking to, at the very most beat him up. But what I saw was so much worse than that.

Have you ever seen those nature programmes where predators rip a defenceless creature to bits? I've seen plenty, and they're tame compared to what I witnessed then. Heads down, they covered the boy with their own bodies, then came away with bits of him – a leg, an arm, intestines – while gouts of blood erupted in the air like a scarlet geyser. As far away as I was, and as rough as I felt, I could still see it way too clearly now. One of the group held up what could only be the kid's head, then chomped into his cheek like it was a watermelon, while another man nourished himself on the tendons dangling down from the neck, the blood pouring over his face.

That was it, I felt a lurch in my stomach and suddenly I was on my hands and knees vomiting onto the carpet. Breathing deeply, I got a handle on it, then tried to stand again to look back out of the window.

The gang and the youth were gone, leaving behind a stain on the road. And now I came to look, those same stains were everywhere. It was like the first time I'd looked out of the window I'd seen what I'd been expecting to see (the mind can be a funny thing in times of stress). Finally I was being shown the true horror of it all, bit by agonising bit, parts of the puzzle revealed in fragments so I wouldn't go stark, staring mad all in one go.

I snatched up the phone to call the police – the line was dead. Likewise, my mobile was useless and just kept dropping my call. Either everyone was using the system or it had simply overloaded; the pressure of last night's New Year messages coupled with frantic calls reporting murders like the one I'd just seen, still not realising the full implications of it, still thinking the police or the army or whoever would be able to stop them.

I shut my eyes, put my hands over my ears.

It was then, after the ringing sounds grew muffled, that I realised the alarm bells going off weren't in my head at all. They were coming from other flats in my block. Several going off at once. There were intruders, people in the building...

I know that sounds ridiculous to you: people. But that's what I still thought at the time. That somehow the men and women who had killed that young boy and made a feast of him had just been gripped by some mass hysteria which turned them into cannibals – but they were still essentially human. It wasn't until I saw one of them up close and personal that I realised reality and fantasy no longer had any boundaries. That the world we'd been depicting in films and in books all these years was finally here.

There was a banging on my door. I lowered my hands and stepped back against the wall, almost slipping in the puddle of my own sick.

Another bang – I won't call it a knock, because it was more than that, it sounded like fists pounding on the door.

I crept towards the noise, quietly; stupid thing to do I know, but I had to see whether it was one of those... those maniacs, or someone who just needed help. I inched towards the peephole, pressing my face against the wood. Something pressed itself up against it on the other side. No, not pressed; was rammed, at high speed. I flinched, but didn't look away. I saw an eye, then a squashed nose and mouth as a woman's face slid down the peephole, leaving a red streak. Then it was gone, yanked back. And I saw the thing that was holding her. Its skin was kind of grey, and I didn't have to touch it to know it was stone cold. Flaps of the rubbery stuff hung off at the forehead and chin revealing yellowing bone beneath. Clumps of its hair had fallen out; what was left was thin and matted with mud. In life it had been a man, but the only way I could really tell was because it wore a suit, which was loose on its frame. One of its eyes was missing, leaving only a gaping hole in its head. And I could see black insects crawling around at the shirt collar.

It held the woman with one hand, the strength it must have taken incredible. Then it shoved her forwards into my door again with tremendous force. This time I saw the woman's teeth splinter and the peephole was totally obscured. Now I did move back from the door as the banging continued. It hadn't been someone wanting to get inside, but another murder – and this time I couldn't ignore what I'd seen. Couldn't rationalise it, either. Her attacker had been dead. I don't need to use the 'Z' word, we all know it, especially now. And it did at least explain what had happened to the youth outside.

I was petrified, as you can imagine, but it didn't stop me trying to figure it all out. I guess everyone was the same the first time they saw it, couldn't believe it, then wanted to know: how? How could the dead be walking around like us? You go through all the possible explanations, don't you? You can probably tick them off one by one with me. Biological warfare – some foreign power had finally gone and done it, produced a weapon that would turn our own deceased against us. There were plenty of them messing about with chemicals, it stood to reason that eventually one combination would do something like this. There was even the possibility that it wasn't happening at all, that someone had released some weird hallucinogen and we were seeing things that we knew could only exist in our imagination. I remembered the woman and the door, the youth on the street, and shook my head. No, that had been real, surely... Why imagine that, out of all the things your brain could come up with?

Had our own scientists been working on bringing back the dead, then? Perhaps behind locked doors – you hear of cloning dinosaurs, time travel, why not this? Maybe some of them escaped and spread the infection?

Pat yourself on the back if you went for a meteor as the next possible answer: a comet that didn't send us blind this time, it just reanimated our dead. Spores travelling through space in the hopes of landing somewhere and coaxing corpses back from their final resting places.

I started to think of more and more stupid explanations – had the Grim Reaper quit or been fired, and as a revenge undone all his previous work? Maybe the dead simply got fed up of being in the ground, decided they wanted back into the land of the living? Or Heaven and Hell were now too full and were turning the dead back out.

Was this what they'd always talked about in the Bible? Judgement Day? Naw, who'd believe something like that?

All these thoughts went round in my head as

I retreated back into my flat, well away from the door. The banging had stopped now and in my mind I pictured what might be happening on the other side of that barrier – the dead man tucking into the woman's brains, her skull cracked wide open. I don't know how long I waited there in the living room, biting my lip and wondering what to do next, but the alarms eventually faded away when nobody responded to them.

I checked the TV, to see if there was any information about what had happened. Nothing, not even the expected announcement from some guy behind a desk with big glasses telling you what you already know. No BBC, no ITV, Channels 4 or 5. The satellite stations had no signal; whether any of this was a local or global problem, I had no way of knowing. There was still music on the radio, though – only problem was that it was being played on a loop with no DJ in-between offering any kind of hope. Just the sound of another person's voice would have been something at least.

I took another look out of the window, keeping to one side in case anyone should see me. The streets were still empty. *Were there any living people left out there?* I wondered. If it was true and they were what I suspected – the evidence was definitely stacking up – those who were still alive would be outnumbered by *them*, and just how do you kill something that's already dead? We've been told that a shot to the head usually works, but the police and the army all had guns and there was no sign of them here. That was another thing they'd got wrong.

By the time it started to get dark, I was feeling hungry and pretty dehydrated. I'd tried to drink water but it just came back up. And my cupboards were pretty much bare after both Xmas and New Year. I knew I would have to venture out of my "safe" haven at some point, I couldn't stay there forever. But sheer terror kept me inside.

In the end the decision was taken out of my hands.

At about eight o clock that night I smelt smoke. I staggered to the door, still a little dizzy, and sure enough I could see wisps of it creeping underneath. I felt the wood and it wasn't hot, so I knew the fire wasn't immediately outside. But it was somewhere close. I tried to see through the peephole, but the dried-on blood made it all but impossible.

Behind me, the smoke detector in the living room started beeping. I climbed on a chair, just like I do when I sometimes burn the toast, and pressed the switch to calm it. The beeping didn't stop, because it wasn't just a dodgy toaster this time. It was telling me there was real danger if I stayed in my flat, that if I remained here the dead people would be the least of my concerns. But the beeping was going through me; I ripped the detector off the ceiling, got down and stamped on it, then felt guilty because it was only trying to keep me safe. Totally crazy, I know, but my emotions were all over the place by this time.

The smoke was growing thicker. I had to either get out now while I still could, or breathe it all in and get it over with. *Better than being eaten*, I thought. But as I started to cough, some sort of survival instinct I didn't know I had took over. I went to the kitchen and pulled the longest, sharpest knife out of the rack – I didn't know what protection this was going to offer me from *them*, but figured it was better than nothing. The window was too high to climb out of, my flat being on the fifth floor, so I had no choice but to go out through the front door.

Tentatively, I undid the Yale lock, flicking up the switch. I brought out a handkerchief and held it to my mouth to stop myself from coughing again and giving away my presence to anyone on the other side.

Carefully, I opened the door a crack, and a gout of smoke pushed its way inside my flat, trespassing. I couldn't see that much out on the landing, but there didn't seem to be anyone there – dead or alive. I was left with little choice anyway. Now that the smoke was in my place too, I had to try and get out of the building. Wafting away the black tendrils as best I could, I made my way across the landing. The smoke was coming from somewhere down the hall. Maybe someone had tried to set one of those things alight at some point, or had just left something cooking on a hob and gone out to investigate what was going on – then never returned? It didn't really matter anyway, I could feel the heat of a fire that was spreading through a place I used to call home.

I headed for where I thought the stairs should be, not about to risk the lift. I kept the hankie over my nose and mouth, but my eyes were stinging. Some of the doors I passed to the other flats were open, some were hanging off their hinges – I guess I had been lucky; I'd never been safe in there at all. Now it really was time to get out. I found the door to the stairs and attempted to pull the handle, though it wasn't easy holding the knife as well.

There was a hand on my shoulder, which spun me around. I dropped my weapon.

Through tear-stained eyes I squinted at the figure looming large in front of me. Its features were obscured by the smoke at first, but when it moved closer I could see it was one of my neighbours from up the hall, a man in his thirties with wavy chestnut hair. I'd seen him around – of course I had, even shared a lift with him once – but never really had the guts to talk to him before now.

"Oh, thank God!" were his first words, coughed out, spluttered. "Do you know what's happening?"

I snatched up the knife again. "No, but we have to get out of here, it's danger—"

His eyes grew wide with fear and he raised his finger, backing away. Before I could turn, I was knocked out of the way by the doors to the stairs opening suddenly. Several bodies swept through and they lunged at the man, pushing him back into the smoke. I saw quick flashes – a pair of scabby hands at his neck, others reaching out for him – then I heard the screams and gurgles as they sank their teeth into his flesh. (Story of my life with guys; easy come, easy go.) One member of the group had stayed behind the rest, a fat bald man with a moustache. Except that the closer I looked, the more I could tell he wasn't naturally fat, it was just that his stomach – which was hanging over his trousers – was painfully distended. He turned and looked right at me, with glazed-over eyes that were seeing me, but couldn't really see. Opening his mouth, he let out a slow and disturbing moan. Then he came towards me.

"Stay back," I warned, slashing the knife through the smoke. The man cocked his head but kept on coming, ignoring the blade completely.

"I said stay back!" This time I slashed at him, catching his raised hands with the knife. There was no blood where the cuts appeared, just a kind of black sludge that dripped down his palms onto the floor. He kept on coming, then slipped in the pool of his own juice, sliding sideways into the wall. I saw my chance and stepped over him, missing his clutching fingers by centimetres. I didn't hesitate with the door this time, straight open and through. I stumbled down the first flight, almost slipping on a few steps until I found my balance.

I didn't come across any more of them on the stairs, thank God, but did see more smoke coming from the lower levels. At the first available ground-floor exit, I pushed down on the handle and stumbled out onto the street. It was night-time and there were precious few streetlamps working; they were either smashed or had simply died. Pity there was no hope of resurrecting those. I had to rely on the glow from a moon that looked – quite appropriately – like somebody had taken a bite out of it. I ran from the block of flats and, looking up, could see the fire's glow from the windows. It was spreading quickly and would soon gut the whole building.

I kept to the shadows and saw more fires here and there on the streets. But where should I be heading? The glib answer came back: the mall. I ignored that, seeing as the nearest one to us was in the next city, though if I could find one of the stores with the smashed-in windows I would also find some food. I was getting very hungry now and it was fairly cold out here on this winter's evening. I hadn't had time to grab a coat, hadn't really thought about it to be honest, and my jumper was pretty thin. I hugged myself to keep in what was left of the warmth, but it didn't do much good.

I've always been a bit scared of the dark, ever since I was a little girl – and now every sound on those streets was magnified. It made for a terrifying combination. What I wouldn't have given to have that light back from the morning, at least then I could see what was coming after me. Mind you, having seen some of them only inches away I did wonder which was worse. I passed more abandoned cars and, not for the first time that night, I wished I'd kept up my driving lessons when I'd had the chance – it would be no good waiting at the bus stop anymore in the hope that a double decker would take me away from all this.

I sought refuge in the local mini-mart, trying a back-door and finding it open. There was a light on somewhere inside as I crept through into the shop itself, passing doors that must have led to the storerooms or back offices. Slipping as quietly as I could through strips of plastic acting as a partition, I scanned the interior, the harsh strip lighting blinking and dim. It was obvious I hadn't been the only one with this idea: the shelves of those four or five aisles had been ransacked, there were tins on the floor, dented like somebody had hit them with something, remnants of loaves of bread, fruit and vegetables squashed as they'd been trampled on.

There wasn't much left, but then beggars couldn't be choosers, I supposed. I found an untouched bag of crisps, ready salted, and scoffed them down – likewise, a packet of digestive biscuits. I was partway through these when I heard a plopping sound coming from my right. I froze. Turning my head sideways, I couldn't see any of the figures I'd been expecting – rather, the noise was coming from the chiller section. The fridges must have packed up at some point during the previous night, because the meat there – bacon, pork chops, liver, chicken – was defrosting under the lights. Not only that, the nearer I drew to it, the more it became obvious that the meat was moving on its own. Those cuts which were open to the air were crawling – yes, crawling! – over each other in an attempt to get out of the fridge. It was this that was making the noise, as the meat dripped onto the floor of the mini-mart and made its way, caterpillar-like, over the shiny surface. The same thing was happening with the fish, too, scaly trout flapped around on their beds of green garnish, dead eyes watching me accusingly. The boxes of eggs, were also tipped onto the floor – and the whites and yolks were fusing together to create some new creature in death; the chick embryos, nowhere near fully formed, wanted a taste of the life that had been denied them.

Watching the meat inching towards me made me feel ill again, and I struggled to keep down the crisps and biscuits, failing miserably. If what I'd seen earlier on had been hard to take in, this was so much worse. Whatever had brought back all those dead human beings hadn't stopped there. *Anything* dead was fair game, it seemed. It didn't matter whether it had been in the ground or frozen solid, large or small, or just barely organic; nothing escaped it.

More noises, this time from the back of the mini-mart. A figure came through the plastic strips, holding something in its hands. It was the sharpened end of a broom, sticky with gunk. The man was middle-aged with greying hair, wearing spectacles, and two or three more figures came through behind him; a ghastly thin woman who would have given some of the dead out there a run for their money, and a couple of children; a girl aged maybe eleven and a boy, eight. I didn't recognise them so they didn't go to my school – probably private? The youngest child was holding his arm, though, blood pouring from a huge gash there... no, not a gash.

A bite.

The man looked left and right, holding the broom like a rifle, before his eyes settled on me. "Look what they've done, Mary. Look what those fuckers have done to our place!" I couldn't tell whether he was talking about the looters or the dead people. I have to admit I do most of my weekly shop on the way back from school at the supermarket, so I had no idea who these people were but I assumed they must have been holed up in a flat above the mart. Though from the looks of things they must have come down at least once for the boy to have gotten bitten.

The owner waved his makeshift spear in my

direction, and I brought up my knife. Not as effective as his weapon at a distance, but I was hoping it would make him think twice.

"I don't know if you've noticed, mister, but there are more things to worry about than the state of your shop." I nodded at the meat and eggs on the floor.

The older girl screamed out loud. The father jabbed his stick in my direction, a little too close for comfort. "Get out! Get out right now!"

Friendly, I thought. *The whole town – and for all I know, the world – has gone to Hell in a handbasket, or even a shopping basket, and he's taking the mess his shop is in out on me...*

"Listen," I started, but he jabbed that stick at me again. I tumbled backwards, almost into one of the shelves. "For God's sake, I'm not the enemy!"

"Arthur!" shouted the woman, and I thought at first she was telling him to back off. But it was a warning. The little boy was running towards his father – I assumed he was the father – and climbed up on his back. Startled, he whirled around, trying to dislodge the kid but not having much luck. The older girl ran to help pull her brother off, but he kicked her away. Then the boy bit into the man's neck, ripping away tendons and smearing all three of them in redness. The man dropped his stick and fell backwards, but the boy still didn't let go. The once-frozen meat, sensing that there was a victim on hand, slithered towards the man, crawling onto him as he thrashed about. What it would do without teeth, I had no idea, and I didn't want to find out.

I turned and ran, towards the front of the shop this time – not really caring if anyone saw me. The glass was smashed in several places, so I could get out easily enough. What stopped me in my tracks was a gathering of figures outside the shop. At first there were only one or two, then a handful, like the group that had chased the young man that morning. More soon joined them, a dozen or so, emerging from the semi-darkness. As they came nearer and the fluorescent lighting of the shop caught them, I could see many variations, from one man who was completely naked, the skin pock-marked and decayed, to one that was ancient and bony, dust and rags falling from its body as it shuffled into position. And then one more figure, barely there at all, formed out of ash and dirt with deep pockets of black for eyes. Just as they didn't warn you in horror flicks about the meat, so it was that they hadn't taken into consideration what might happen to those people who hadn't been buried. Not everyone chose to rot away in a casket beneath the earth – some were fried in furnaces, crushed down into ash and kept in urns, or scattered to the winds. What I was looking at was one such creature, made up of powder and dust, that had somehow reformed itself into some semblance of a man.

There they all waited, growing in numbers by the second – like they could communicate telepathically and let others know. In no time there were at least fifty of them.

How was I going to get past them? They'd be on me in a matter of seconds if I went out the front. As before in the flat I wasn't left with much of choice, because they stormed the frontage almost as one, breaking down the rest of the glass, cuts meaning nothing to them. I tried to turn again, to run in the other direction, but they swarmed all over me. I lashed out with my knife, hitting first one body, then another. Their combined moans were deafening.

I was carried backwards through the shop,

where the man was still wrestling with his son. The wife and daughter didn't get a chance to run, they were grabbed by several of the dead at once – one of their attackers having what looked like a dislocated shoulder, another wore a hospital gown with blood staining the front where some stitches must have come open (or had he actually died on the operating theatre when this happened?). The whole scene became a frenzy of biting, of clutching hands and screaming. Like me, they fell beneath the sea of decaying bodies. There was nothing I could do for them, or even myself. There was no air now, no room to move – it would only be a matter of moments before they started to bite into me. I had to face it, I was dead.

I have to tell you, I've never been so thankful in my life for anything as I was right then when I finally passed out.

~

For a long, long time blackness was all I knew.

Waking from that was the hardest thing I can ever remember. I really didn't want to come round... I ached worse than I had on New Year's morning, but at least that pain meant I was still alive... didn't it? I opened my eyes slowly; it wasn't *that* much lighter. I didn't know where I was, but I definitely wasn't in the mini-mart. Again I was relying on the moon for light, now streaming in through – not a window, but a square hole in the wall. Was it still the same night, or had another 24 hours passed? I had no way of knowing; in my rush to get out of the flat, I'd left my watch as well... But I did know I'd woken even hungrier than before, a consequence of not eating for at least a day and spewing my guts up twice now.

It was cold and smelt musty. I raised myself up and found that I wasn't on the floor, but resting on something hard a few feet above the ground. My knife was gone. I swung myself around and my legs dangled over the edge, with something hard pressing into the backs of my knees. Quickly, I checked my arms, my legs and my neck for bites. There was nothing.

I couldn't work it out. Why was I still alive? Why, when they'd ripped that youth to shreds, when they'd eaten my neighbour and killed the family back there in the mini-mart? By rights I should have been a meal for that horde back there. Had someone rescued me at the last minute, were there more survivors that hadn't been murdered and devoured?

The other thing I couldn't work out was where I'd ended up. The surface I was sitting on was freezing. I checked my pockets, glad now that I'd broken my cigarette fast and kept my matches about my person. I took one out and struck it against the side of the box. The room, or at least the area immediately surrounding me, burst into light. I held up the match, knowing that I didn't have long before it burnt down to my fingers. The walls were made of stone, mossy even here on the inside, and I was sitting on stone as well.

I jumped off, almost toppling over and breaking my ankle as I struggled to find my feet and my balance at the same time. I'd been sitting on a lid of some kind, I could see the edges where it overhung. But a lid to what? Bending down, I could see carvings on that lid, but my match burnt out before I could have a proper look. I lit another quickly and was confronted by a face only centimetres from mine. I drew in a frightened breath. The face had no eyes – actually that wasn't strictly true. It had eyes, it's just that they were blind, white and smooth with no pupils. The face was alabaster too with not a blemish to be seen, hair – also white – in curls framing that same face. I was looking at an angel. And the angel was looking back.

In fact, there were two – one on either side of this tomb, guarding the dead. But they weren't doing a very good job of it, because I noticed that the lid I'd been on wasn't quite as flush as I thought. There was a gap on the left hand side, fingers poking out. There was a grinding sound as the fingers inched away that lid, as heavy as it was.

I backed away as the light faded from my match. I fumbled for another one while the rumbling sound continued. When I struck it, I was confronted with the thing from the tomb; as white as the angels, but there the similarities ended. This poor sod was covered in cobwebs, covered in spiders too, but what little of his features I saw were hideous. Slack-faced, eyes so much jelly, when he raised his skeletal arms the webs came with them, so that it looked for all the world like he had wings. Not angel wings, more a demon's. Grinning, he pinched out the match.

I felt his hands on me, gripping my

shoulders. *Is this why they'd brought me here?* I thought – *to be a sacrifice to this interred thing, unable or unwilling to leave his home?*

I kicked out, and my foot connected with its midriff. He let go and I seized my chance to get away, running and striking another match as I went – my last one. There was a door, a huge wooden thing, but it was closed. And there was no handle.

Frantically, I searched around for something I could lever it open with – but there was nothing. I banged on the door, crying to be let out. In the dimness, I saw the white shape coming towards me again. There was that moaning sound they all made, a guttural, almost choking sound. Just when I thought that was it, the door opened from the outside and I fell back into someone's arms.

They lifted me up, and closed the door at the same time, shutting out the moans from behind. I was pulled backwards and caught a glimpse of the mausoleum I'd been trapped inside; in life the creature must have had pots of money because the place was like a small shrine to him, with intricate carvings that caught the light from the moon.

My match had gone out by this time, but I didn't need it to see now. I was amongst a group of people: men, women and children. "Are you okay?" asked a woman with frizzy hair.

"Give her some room," said the square-jawed man who'd dragged me out of there. He had what appeared to be a hooked poker in his hand.

They must have been one of the few surviving local groups, I reasoned, banded together for survival.

"We followed a bunch of them from town, and saw them bring you here..." another woman explained. But where *was* here exactly? I looked around and took in more of the scene; gravestones, monuments, more angels. Though I hadn't had much call to visit – my own, adoptive, parents were buried some 150 miles away (and the further away the better as far as I was concerned) – I knew the town had one major graveyard, attached to the grounds of St Benjamin's Church. The church was where the interminable school carol services were held every single year, including a couple of weeks ago, but I'd never hung around long enough to explore the grounds. "We've come to take as many of them out as we can in one go," she explained, pointing to the cans of petrol most of the group were carrying. I knew now who'd been setting the fires around town, maybe even in my block of flats?

"I think we're all that's left," said another member of the gang, "we have to stick together."

I nodded. As they led me through the grounds, we kept low, hiding behind graves and moving like they do in those old war films. I could see the earth disturbed at each and every one of those graves, where the dead had somehow dug up through the soil to escape. At the heart of the graveyard, the man who'd saved me signalled for us all to halt. He waved with his hand and I followed where he was indicating. There, amongst the headstones, was a massive group of them – gnawing on what was left of another feast. One was even licking his fingers like he was enjoying a Kentucky Fried Chicken meal!

"When I give the word," whispered my rescuer – I still didn't know his name, "douse them."

"I... I'm not so sure this is a good idea," I said.

The man stared at me, shaking his head.

"We should get away, while we still can – I've seen what..."

"Don't just stand there, grab her," he snapped to the people on either side of me.

"What? What're you..." The woman who'd explained the plan grabbed my left arm, and a man on my other side held me by the right.

"Shut her up," said my former rescuer. I could sort of see his point – the dead were turning away from their scraps to the fresh meat. They started moaning, loudly, drawing more of their kind to this central place.

The game up, Mr Square Jaw gave an instruction to toss me over to the dead. I tried to wrench my arms away, but they held me fast – then more hands came to help and threw me over a tombstone in amongst the corpses. I couldn't believe what was happening; they'd rescued me from the thing in the mausoleum only to use me as a distraction while they attacked! What's more, it seemed to be working...

The dead reached down for me, grabbing with ice-cold hands. "No, get off!" I cried, but they kept on clutching.

At the same time, the survivors launched into their attack – spraying petrol everywhere. The smell reached me and I gagged. Dragged up to standing position, I waited a second time for the zombies – there, I've said it – to tuck into me. Again, they didn't, they just made that incessant moaning noise.

The first wave rolled over the people with the cans, ignoring the stink of gasoline – after all, they smelt much, much worse themselves. More came, then still more, surrounding me... and, in a strange sort of way, protecting me.

For the first time that day I felt an odd kind of safety. The dead weren't biting me, they weren't eating me.

They were trying to communicate...

I looked down and saw the little boy from the mini-mart, the one who'd been turned. He let out a grotesque mewl. Then he took my hand. I gaped at it in disbelief and confusion.

The zombies swarmed over the survivors, who were totally outnumbered. The only thing they had to their advantage was fire. The man who'd rescued me flicked open a silver zippo which glinted in the moonlight.

I looked from the boy to the man.

"No," I said. Then I let go of the boy and ran at my rescuer. Was this revenge for what he'd done? Kind of. But it was more about stopping him from doing the stupidest thing he'd ever do. Fire wouldn't stop them, it never could – reduce them to ash and they'd still come back, I'd seen that for myself. I guess some part of me was trying to prevent a sacrifice that wouldn't work. "I can't let you do it."

I slapped the lighter from his hand and it fell to the floor, going out as it did so. He brought the poker round in an arc, catching me on the shoulder. I felt nothing. Then I put my hands around his neck. "Don't you see... You can't win! You could *never* win." I felt his bones breaking as he dropped to his knees. I took a certain amount of satisfaction from that, picturing all the worthless men who'd ever let me down, all the broken relationships that hadn't been my fault.

The zombies had incapacitated the rest of the survivors, biting into them, swallowing gleefully. I watched, then remembered how very hungry I still was.

"No..." gasped the man, barely audible.

I smiled, then bit into his face.

~

You see, it all makes sense when you think about it – their mindset, their philosophy. It's a way of creating a wholeness the likes of which the world has never seen before, a unity in death, even for those who are eaten. They contribute to the cycle, they live on within us.

Oh, that's right: I also forgot to mention one small detail – probably because I couldn't remember myself until those final few moments when I looked into that man's eyes. I'm dead myself. Have been ever since New Year's Eve, when I couldn't stand the noise of the parties going on all around, fireworks outside, and I… I had nothing to keep me company but a full bottle of vodka and far too many pills. I've never really been a people person, and even the kids at school hated me, I could tell. Not like the children who will live forever in my extended family now.

And they're not meaningless moans at all, the noises that they make – the noises that *I* made as I tried to talk to the man back at my block of flats, the people from the mini-mart, my rescuers; which was why they suddenly turned as they did, spurning me as everyone else has done in my life. The moans and groans are just a different kind of language; you just have to listen properly. Oh, and be dead, of course. We're not telepathic, but we do talk a lot; we're all very, very close.

I still don't know what caused any of this, so don't ask me. All I know is that I'm happy. Finally, *truly* happy. What more can anyone ask? I'm still Helen Kirby, inside. Doesn't matter what I look like now that I've started to decompose. I'm immortal, just like the skeletal figures, just like my friend back there from the tomb – who was also trying to show me the error of my ways. Just like the ash-corpses.

Soon there will be no one like you left and the world will belong to us. The dead. This is where they usually say it, isn't it? The End? When the movie's finished.

Except this is never going to end. Not really. This is real life, this is the time of the dead. And although they got some of the things right in films.

They got just as many oh, so wrong.

Dead Reckoning

Hi, I'm David Hawthorne – Dave to my friends – and I'm a dead man.

Not in the way your wife (or in my case, partner) might once have said it if you got home late – not that I've ever been one for staggering back at all hours – or someone from the old days threatening you in a fight. I've never been much for brawling either. I was always being told by my parents growing up: *use your brains instead, David, use your brains*. So that's what I did. I used what I had – studied hard, got decent grades, got into Uni, though it was a toss-up at that time between the sciences (I was pretty good at chemistry) and history. In the end I plumped for anthropology, which allowed me to incorporate history into my...

Sorry, I'm lecturing. Old habit... maybe

because that's what I ended up doing with my life; lecturing the subject that I studied. Never really finding my way out of the academic trenches, stuck in my own little further education world. My own little kingdom, Natalie used to call it – and maybe she was right. I was quite a respected lecturer, even if it was only on a casual basis at the local college. The students – my 'loyal subjects' – seemed to love my classes, probably because I tried to put them at ease, tried to make things enjoyable for them. Anthropology is, after all, the study of them. Of *us*.

Not that we're really us anymore, are we? I'm assuming you're the same as me, or you wouldn't even be able to understand what I'm saying, I don't think. None of them do really, no matter how much you talk, how eloquent the language – they just hear the usual. Our *new* language, I suppose...

Not quite sure what a study of us would be called now. Necropology? The way I figure it, we're the next stage in evolution. We're different; we're *better*. That makes us sound like X-Men or something. God, nothing could be farther from the truth. It's taken me a long time to even come to terms with what I am, with what I see in the mirror or in reflections from windows and shop storefronts.

But anyway, enough – your heart bleeds, right? Maybe even literally. We've all got to deal with things in our own way. But I'm here to tell you my story, to let you know what happened to me, and how I got to be in this position. Some people think I'm crazy for doing this, but getting the word out has got to start somewhere. After I'm done you can decide what you want to do. Join us or... You might not approve of everything you hear, but I do have my reasons for the things I've done.

Okay, so, New Year's Eve. That was when it happened, as I'm sure a lot of you already know. Sometime overnight, after midnight, definitely – because I was... Right, I'll start at the beginning. I was spending New Year's alone that year after a massive bust up with Nat, following the debacle that was Christmas Day with her parents. Or, as I liked to call them, the mutants. Talk about a day with the living dead, and that was *before* whatever happened, happened. Of course, Nat wouldn't hear a word against them as usual – not even after they made dig after dig about my chosen line of work. "When are you thinking of getting a proper job?" was one of the remarks her mother was fond of making. A proper job? Just because I wasn't full-time at a posh university, and what hours I did have were in danger of being reduced by the latest round of government cuts. "Nat earns twice as much as you do," was another one, this time from her father. Course she did, working in advertising, but it was money for old rope. (I never said this to Nat; not often at any rate.)

Christ, and to think I might've ended up marrying into that family. I reckon I had a lucky escape. But I do... *did* love Nat. As long as I'm being honest, though, I always thought she was too good for me. Maybe she thought so as well, a bit. She was pretty, bright... what on earth was she doing with me? But we worked, or so I thought. Worked well enough for it to have lasted four years, anyway – the longest I'd ever been with anyone.

We met at a book fair. She was there for pleasure, I was tracking down a rare volume of a book I needed for my research, for yet another dry textbook I was trying to get published. At one stall, we both reached for the same book at the same time, and our fingers brushed. I thought stuff like that only happened in movies – and crappy chick flicks at that. So did Nat, as it turned out, and we both laughed about it over a coffee as we chatted.

We saw each other a few times after that, for meals or a drink or to see a film. I told her about my working class background. I'm not one to whine about my poor origins, though; I'd been happy enough. Even when the TV broke and we couldn't afford another, I was content listening to the radio. Preferred it, actually, tuning in to radio serials about spaceships and aliens. The family? All gone... all dead...

(Not now, of course. That word has a different meaning after New Year's. Let's just say they'd been 'resting' then.)

...Mum from a massive stroke when I was in my early twenties, Dad from emphysema after working down the mines all his life – that had only been a couple of years before I met Nat. Hers, however, were still very much alive. Still very much with us... a lot. Especially after we moved in together, coming round and interfering. If *I* thought Nat wasn't good enough for me, then they were certain of it. "Should have stuck with that lovely Timothy Nesbit, he was perfect for you," her mother would remark – and with me sitting there as well. She even brought photos round of Nat with Tim, in an old family album, and expected me to look at them. I never kept any photos of my old girlfriends; didn't want the reminders. I'd smile – *grimace* – as Nat and her mother went down memory lane and talked about all the nice times Tim had spent with the clan. "Fitted right in, he did," Nat's mother would say and then cast me that disdainful look over her shoulder, as if she couldn't believe I was even indoors, let alone on the furniture. "And he's doing very well now, you know. Tipped to take over the entire company someday." Yeah, *his father's* company. Wonder how that happened? He'd be head honcho, king of the castle. Only his little plan didn't really work out, did it?

So, you see, there was precedent. I didn't only have to put up with all that for the one day. For Christmas Day. The argument I had with Nat over her folks had been building for some time. Oh, but it was a big one. I even called her mum a "complete bitch", which did not go down at all well... but it was true. It ended up with Nat throwing the presents I'd bought her back at me, and one of them was a foot spa-massager. That really hurt when it whacked me on the arm. She had a bit of a fiery temper when she got going, did Nat. Then she stormed out, screaming that she hated me, and took a taxi to her parents' place. I tried ringing a few times over the holidays but her mobile was always off and they refused to put her on when I rang the landline. "She doesn't want to speak to you," her cow of a mother would snort. I didn't know whether it was Nat or just her parents talking, but either way I couldn't get through to talk it out with her calmly. That's what I like to do, you see. Usually. Talk things through.

In any event, it left me all on my own come New Year's Eve. We were planning on spending it at home, snuggled up on the couch watching the celebrations on TV, counting down the minutes till midnight and having a kiss – then hopefully more – to see in the next twelve months. But those plans didn't work out, either.

After not getting through on the phone again – this time they didn't even pick up – I took myself off to the pub. I'm not usually one for drinking heavily either, but while the rest of the crowds there were cheering, I had sorrows to drown. How little I knew. I had a few pints and chasers, enough to get me nicely merry, as my dad used to call it – sitting in the corner, people watching. By the time the bells were chiming and couples were hooking up at midnight, I'd had enough.

I left The Crown and began my steady walk – or stagger – home, cursing the fact that the cool night air was sobering me up a little. I think I must have got a bit lost, because I remember thinking that the streets didn't look familiar. I'd taken a wrong turn somewhere. I retraced my steps, and quickly realised I needed to cross the road. Looking left and right, I stepped off the pavement.

Then it happened.

The car came out of nowhere – and I think the driver must have been out drinking as well, because he or she was all over the place. Then it was as if they were aiming for me. I don't remember much about the car, the make or anything, but I do remember it being red. I could see that much in the light from the streetlamps. I thought to myself, *my blood's not going to even stain that bloody thing! Not even when it's spraying all over the bonnet.*

And next thing I was seeing that bonnet up close and personal, the bumper hitting me at speed, pitching me up in the air. They say at moments like that, your entire life flashes before your eyes. Mine didn't; but everything *did* slow down.

Then time sped up again, and I was rolling off – hitting the concrete and blacking out. I barely had time to feel the pain before everything just blinked out, like someone tugging on a cord to turn off a bathroom light.

And the cord was pulled again – several times. Black, white, black, white... Or more accurately the yellow-orange glow of the streetlamp nearby. I was lying strangely, that much I could tell – like when you wake up and you have a crick in your neck and your arms and legs feel like they don't belong to you. I blinked a few more times and then my eyes stayed open. Turning my head, I expected to feel something: a jarring jolt of pain, bones protesting, nerve-endings screaming out. But there was nothing. I looked down at the arm by my side, my legs out at strange angles. The whole of my body still felt numb. I tried to move my hands. Nothing. Tried to shift the position of my legs. Again, nothing.

Holy shit, I thought, *I'm paralysed from the neck down!*

No. I wasn't going to let that happen. Mind over matter, I told myself, that's all it was. I wasn't going to end up in some wheelchair, being spoon-fed. I looked down the length of my body, and willed my limbs to move. Even if it was only a twitch of my little finger, it would be enough. Proof that I wasn't going to spend the rest of my days like this.

Come on, come on... give me something...

There! My foot jerked. It took all my concentration on that one spot at first, but I felt both my foot and leg move. Then it was my hand and arm. Again, I was expecting this to hurt – I'd been run over, after all – but it didn't, and I managed to get an elbow underneath myself, rolling over so I could try and get up. It was quite a process, but I managed to lever myself into a sitting position. My head was on my shoulder, so I straightened it out and winced as I heard bones crack. I remember thinking: *that* can't *be good*. But there still wasn't any pain, so I continued with my mission to stand. It never occurred to me that I might be in shock or something, that the accident might have done so much damage I might never feel anything *again*. I suppose I rationalised it by remembering the alcohol I'd had, wondering if that could have numbed the pain, and when it wore off I'd feel like warmed-over dog crap.

I just wanted to get up, to prove to myself I wasn't crippled. To challenge the evidence of my eyes.

There was another loud cracking sound as I straightened, pulling my scuffed long coat out of the way, getting onto my knees first and then shuffling over to the nearby lamppost like *Toulouse Lautrec*, to use it for support. I pulled myself up and heard more cracks, my body protesting at such treatment. My head lolled again and I straightened it – more sounds, like guns going off in my skull. I suppose that's why I didn't really hear the noise at first. The real sound of guns being fired in the distance.

Holding onto the lamppost, I pulled myself around, squinting, my eyes still adjusting. My head was dipped, so I saw the tyre tracks first, leading off down the road. I followed them, looking up and tracing them to the spot where the car had come to grief in the distance. After hitting me, the driver had mounted the pavement, wheels churning up the grass verges, before ploughing the front end into another lamppost like the one I was leaning against. Even from here I could see the vehicle was a write-off; there was smoke coming from somewhere and the front end had branched off into two bits, hugging the concrete of the post – which didn't look too stable itself.

Blinking again, I attempted a few experimental steps on my own. The first couple I took quickly, holding out my arms to get my balance. I nearly ended up pitching forward onto the concrete, but managed to save myself. I must have looked like Bambi on the ice... if Bambi had been a grown college lecturer mown down by a drunk driver.

Walking became easier once I'd learned where my centre of gravity was, but all the same it was an effort to make it down the road, to check out the wreckage. I'm not entirely sure I wanted to help – this person had just knocked me down for heaven's sake, almost killed me (that's a good one now, looking back). I think I was just curious, in spite of the potential danger. For one thing the driver's door was open, the glass in it shattered. Of the driver there was no sign.

I felt angry. They'd obviously got out of this with barely a scratch. Climbed out of the car and done a runner before the authorities could arrive to breathalyse and arrest them.

I spotted the blood next, trailing from the driver's doorway, taking up where the tyre tracks had left off. Up the road. I couldn't help a small grin at that. So they *had* been injured, at least? I suddenly felt guilty. Maybe they were so badly injured they'd wandered off up the road looking for medical assistance. I imagined an arm hanging off at the shoulder, or belly ripped open, holding intestines in as they made a bid for the nearest hospital.

I shook my head. Why didn't they just call the emergency services on a mobile? They had to have one; everybody did these days. Even I...

What an idiot! I should have done that myself. Instead of trying to move, to get up, I should have just reached into my pocket, pulled out my good old Motorola and tapped in 999. But you weren't supposed to move people who had neck injuries, were you? It could actually *cause* paralysis. So what about those morons who moved themselves? What would the paramedics and doctors have to say about that?

I didn't care. I took out my phone, thankful for the fact it was still intact after my ordeal, and dialled the number.

It was busy. Frowning, I dialled again... and got the same response. Then I remembered what night it was. The lines were probably jammed up with calls from revellers who'd got themselves into trouble. Kids fighting – maybe even some of my own students? – other people having accidents.

I tried one last time and an automated voice told me that they couldn't connect me to that number. I frowned again.

More smoke was rising from the car, so I decided to distance myself from it in case the thing blew, and followed the trail of blood up and along the street. It was then that I started to become aware of the noises. The bangs, growing louder.

Fireworks, I thought. Somewhere out there were folk whose lives hadn't been turned upside down. Literally, in my case: upside down to land, hard, on concrete. Not the best start to any year. Somewhere out there people were still celebrating the death of one year and the birth of another. Little did I realise, or understand, that it was the death of a way of life I was hearing – and the birth of a new species.

It was as I turned the first corner that I saw signs something wasn't quite right. There was a woman running, purple satin party dress shredded across the front, exposing the left cup of a white lace bra. She had no shoes on, and I reasoned that she must have kicked off her high heels – she had to have been wearing heels with that outfit – in favour of speed. She spotted me, and changed direction, heading towards me. And the closer she got the more I saw of her distress; she'd been crying and her mascara had run down her face in black tears, as if she was weeping pure evil. Her lipstick was smudged, not from kissing, but possibly from some kind of clumsy attempt by someone to claw at her face, her mouth.

"Help me!" she screamed, speeding up. "Oh God, please *help me!*"

I frowned once more. This was the weirdest damn night I'd ever experienced. First the accident, now this. She was only a few metres away when I saw what she was running from. They'd turned a corner up ahead, some kind of mob chasing her. It looked like something out of a comedy programme, though it was anything but funny.

"Help me!" she pleaded again.

It's okay, I wanted to tell her – but it really wasn't. The mob was following, fast, and now that she was heading in my direction, so were they. I wasn't sure I was up to running, but as soon as she was near enough, I grabbed her hand and tried. Putting one foot in front of the other, almost tripping over feet that still felt pretty numb. I looked back, head lolling again more than it probably should have done – but I ignored this. We had other, more pressing, problems. The woman was looking back over her shoulder as well, terrified. And with little wonder: there had to be about thirty, maybe forty or even fifty people in that mob. The mob that was still pursuing us relentlessly through the streets.

Where are the bloody police when you need them? I thought. What was this, some kind of riot that had started overnight? I remembered back to the ones from recent years, the dissatisfaction of the general populous with the current government, protests escalating into violence in the cities, spreading like a virus across the entire land.

Demonstrations against the – lack of – leadership this country had at the moment.

But at New Year's? Wasn't that a time of good will, of good feeling? Not for everyone, it seemed. Maybe these rioters had had a lousy holiday period and got together to loot and pillage their way into this New Year? Who knows...

All I could think was we needed to get out of there, needed to find somewhere to hide. But, when I looked back again, I saw the crowd was gaining on us.

The woman turned to look at me, pure horror in her eyes, then suddenly she was being pulled backwards. I tried to keep hold of her hand, but her fingers slid through mine like they were covered in butter. I stopped, twisting to reach out for her.

Then the crowd piled in, bodies covering her in seconds. It was as if she was drowning in a sea of limbs. I thought about stopping, attempting a rescue, but there were simply too many of them. As I said before, I'm no fighter really – and against those kinds of odds I wouldn't have lasted ten seconds.

The woman hadn't, either.

You should run, I told myself. *Use the diversion, get away while they're busy with her.*

For the second time that night, I felt guilty. Guilty and ashamed. Here I was, a civilised man, and I was going to use this poor woman as a way of escaping. She started screaming again, her cries intensifying, shrieks of agony coming from underneath the mound of writhing flesh. What in Heaven's name were they doing to her? Raping her, torturing her – *or both?*

The cries abruptly stopped. Either she'd blacked out or...

The first people from the mound pulled back, up and away. But they were holding things. At first I thought they were weapons. Then I saw they were parts of the woman. Someone – a teenager who had that whole Goth look thing going on – was holding part of her arm, severed at the elbow. No, not severed. Ripped away... or *bitten* away. Because as I took in more of this, I saw his mouth was dark with blood.

More members of the scrum were rising from it now, and I saw that they weren't just young people, not simply kids in their teens or twenties – some were middle-aged (an overweight woman wearing a pinafore dress, for example, hair tied back in a severe bun; another man in a business suit, what remained of his hair silver at the temples). They held up trophies of their hunt, like savages. Like animals. And I realised that's what this was: a pack of animals, nothing more. Humanity somehow reduced to its basest form. This was no riot... it was madness. Like something from those old SF serials I'd listened to.

I'd seen enough; and besides, they were starting to notice me again. I could do nothing more for the unfortunate woman. As if to emphasise that fact, a man with a beard and hairy arms came away holding her head, the mascara still running, lipstick still smeared. I felt like screaming myself, but held it inside. I turned and made my way as fast as I could from the scene, hoping against hope that the woman would hold their attention long enough for me to put some distance between us.

I looked back a couple of times, to see a handful of people start to come after me... then they stopped and just watched as I went, as if I wasn't worth the trouble. There was still fresh meat back there, so why bother?

I was grateful to the woman for at least

buying me some time. Maybe even time to think, to work out what the fuck was going on.

A helicopter flew past overhead as I turned down an alleyway – then I heard more of the bangs. Except I couldn't tell myself they were fireworks this time; I could *see* the spark of the bullets from that chopper – police or military, had to be – see the muzzle flash as they opened fire, probably on the mob I'd just escaped from. Now I understood why I couldn't get through on the phone, why there was nobody around to protect the woman who was being chased. They were obviously being stretched to capacity, just as they had been during previous riots. And now all those cuts in spending were really being felt, because something very serious had happened. Something unthinkable, while I'd been unconscious back there on the roadside.

It was the same everywhere I went after that: chaos on the streets; hordes like the gang that had chased the woman, hunting people, killing them and... eating them (it made me feel physically sick back then); helicopters and police cars and, closer to the centre of town, jeeps and tanks as well. Why was I heading through the centre of the city? Because all I could think about was Nat, probably locking herself away in her parents' house on the other side of town, staving off these lunatics as best she could. I had to get to her, had to try and save her.

I narrowly avoided several skirmishes between the gangs and those trying to keep order. In one I witnessed police in riot gear attempting to hold back the masses, but being overrun in seconds. Someone opened fire at the swell of figures with a machine gun; it didn't seem to do any good. I even saw shells being launched into the middle of crowds, which sent bodies spiralling up into the air to land – some in pieces – back on the pavements. But they'd still be alive, that was the weird thing. It didn't seem to matter what you did to them, they just kept coming back and coming back... even if it was only a torso crawling, dragging itself along. Or, at the other end of the scale, a pair of legs with no upper half, and no way of seeing where they were going, banging into vehicles, the sides of buildings. What kind of messed up shit was all this?

I've never done drugs, never even smoked – in spite of the amount that was around during my Uni days and at work – so I knew it wasn't some kind of acid flashback. Perhaps I was hallucinating after the knock on the head from the accident? Or had I even woken up at all? Was this part of some nightmarish coma dream or something? What else could I do though, but treat it as real. It certainly felt it.

Eventually, I made it to the street where Nat's parents lived. Quite an exclusive neighbourhood, or had been (Nat had never really wanted for anything growing up). Thankfully, it seemed relatively untouched by the night's events so far, most of the houses quiet and dark, as if the residents had all fled at some point. Taking one last look left and right, I began down the street, walking past cars that were parked there, counting off the numbers until I reached seventeen: 'The Manor'. Typically, Nat's parents' house was white-washed, with bay windows on the ground floor and a neat garden. It couldn't have been any more middle class if it tried, nor any more pretentious. Not that any of that mattered anymore; people across the city – and for all I knew the country, or even the world – were being brought down to the same level by this... this thing that was happening. And we all had to work together to get through it alive. (I have to laugh at that thought sometimes, remembering. How could we ever get through anything *alive*?)

This house was also in darkness, so maybe they'd gone out for a meal earlier on or something? It was New Year's when all was said and done. The garage was locked so I had no idea whether they'd taken Nat's father's Jag out that evening, so I looked through the bay window of the living room. I couldn't see a thing inside, either.

Looking over my shoulder again – by this time I'd got used to the strange noise my neck made when I did that, the creaking of tightened sinew like old leather – I did something really stupid. I began knocking on the front door. It was all I could think of. I'm no burglar, no good at breaking and entering, and I certainly didn't have any kind of key for this place. What else was I supposed to do?

I banged for a good few minutes, and peered through the window again. And yes, there – just the faintest flash of light coming from somewhere deep inside the house. Light where there had been none before. So they *were* hiding out in this place. Now I *had to* find a way inside.

I tried round the back, opening the gate and feeling my way around to the patio and French windows there, hoping they might prove easier to get through. After my efforts at pulling them open failed, I decided a more direct approach would work better. I picked up a stone from the rockery, slamming it hard against the glass. It held for a couple of blows but finally shattered – throwing me back to the accident which already seemed like days ago. Well, the glass shattered enough for me to get my hand in at least, and open the doors properly.

I called out, knowing that the din must surely have scared Nat and her folks. "It's David... Dave!" I shouted. "I came because I was worried. Is anyone there?"

I made my way through the dining room, but still couldn't see anyone around. Similarly, I checked out the living room and the bedrooms, but found the entire house deserted. It was only when I came back down again and was walking through the hallway, that I saw – or should that be *felt*? – the evidence that someone else was present. Something slammed into my back, pitching me forward into the kitchen area, which I'd checked not ten minutes earlier. I stumbled, trying to keep myself steady; I was still having trouble with my balance. Another whack and I went down, landing heavily on my knees.

I was shocked more than anything, certain by this time that I'd made a mistake with the light, that there really wasn't anyone else here. That Nat and her family had made off, same as the other people on this street. But, as I looked up and over, I saw the trapdoor open in the kitchen, Nat standing by it and her mother's head poking out. Her father's wine cellar! I'd completely forgotten about that. He liked to think he was some kind of expert, talking about his collection – when in fact it wasn't big enough to swing a cat down there, really. Big enough for them to hide in, though, and peek out from when I'd knocked on the door. Nat flashed her torch back on, almost blinding me. "It's one of them, from the news!" her mother screeched. "*Kill it!*"

So it must have been Nat's dad behind me, battering me with something. Hadn't they heard me calling out? I held up my hand, partly to block out the light and partly to try and show them that I wasn't one of those animal-people. "It's me, Nat! It's Dave!"

"Kill it!" repeated Nat's bloody stupid mother, and I had to wonder whether she just wanted me dead anyway.

I twisted round, expecting to see the moustached face of Nat's father holding whatever weapon he had aloft. But even just a glimpse revealed that this man was much younger, with darker hair and a bigger frame.

I froze up completely. It was Tim! Tim from the photos, the guy who "fitted right in". So that had been their plan, to invite him over for a cosy New Year's Eve with Nat – rekindle some of those embers, get the son-in-law they'd always wanted instead of the disappointment I so obviously was (not that we were hitched, but you know what I mean). It seemed surreal, that in the midst of all that was happening, I should feel... what? Betrayed, jealous? Wounded?

(But I still didn't feel physically wounded, in spite of the blows from the cricket bat Tim was wielding, about to strike me with again.)

"What's happening up there?" *This* was Nat's father, finally appearing at the trapdoor now that his wife was making way for him. It was enough of a distraction for me to roll sideways and avoid a third smack with the bat.

Grabbing the side of the kitchen island – of course they had to have a breakfast bar at The Manor! – I tried to get myself to my feet, shouting out again: "It's me, it's David! What the hell's wrong with you people?"

Something else struck me on the shoulder, knocking me back. There was a clatter as the toaster landed on the floor. In a warped replay of what had happened on Christmas Day, Nat was suddenly hurling electrical appliances in my direction. "What are you doing?" I demanded, ducking to avoid a sandwich maker, which – I noted with great satisfaction – hit Tim instead.

Grabbing a metal tray, I held this up as a shield and barged my way across to Nat, dropping it once I was close enough and holding her by the shoulders, pinning her so she couldn't chuck anything else. The torch in her hand spun around, creating crazy patterns on the ceiling. "Nat! You have to listen – it's me. It's your..." I was going to say boyfriend, but I didn't know if I was anymore. "It's David. *Your* Dave!" I was virtually screaming this into her face, which I admit was probably not helping calm her down.

Another thump, across the shoulder-blades this time. I let go, turning to see Nat's mother brandishing the tray I'd just discarded. I shifted position before she could get another strike in, but by then Tim was approaching once more, and Nat's father was clambering out of his cellar. Not knowing what else to do, I skirted around the island and out through the kitchen door again, stumbling backwards into the room with the broken French windows. Even if they'd mistaken me for one of those cannibalistic maniacs outside when I was banging on the door or breaking in, surely they weren't in such a state that they couldn't even listen to my explanations?

They followed quickly enough, now *all* carrying weapons: Tim still had his bat, the mother had her tray and Nat's father had a bottle of wine in each hand ready to lob at me. Only Nat had come through with nothing – except the torch.

Which she flashed at me, right into my face again. "Wait..." she said suddenly. *This is it*, I thought. At last, she's come to her senses, recognised me. She began to step forward, lowering the beam a little so I could see her face, and the look of recognition there.

But also of repulsion.

"David?" she whispered. "Dave is that you?"

What had I been trying to tell her all this

time? "Yes. Yes, it's me Nat." I stepped forward, thinking it was safe, but she pulled another horrified face and drew back. Tim got in front of her swinging the bat.

"Dave..." Nat began to sob. "Oh, David."

I couldn't get my head around this at all. Fair enough if she'd chosen Tim over me, he seemed much better at protecting her anyway, to my chagrin, but why the look on her face? Why wouldn't she even talk to me, tell me outright what she was feeling?

"We should just put it out of its misery," Nat's mother piped up.

And I thought she was rude before! Now not only was the mutt not welcome indoors, but it also needed putting down apparently.

"Quick, before it's too late." This was Nat's father. "Before... before he bites."

Bites?

Tim began to move forward, hefting the bat. And for a moment I just thought, get on with it. Knock me senseless and perhaps when I come round again things will be back to normal, and all this will make sense.

But instead everything went crazy again.

Noises at the front door, and behind in the

kitchen. The quartet looked about them, not sure what was happening. *I* knew, though. All the racket we'd been making had finally attracted the thing they were hiding from. Finally the scourge had made it out here to their exclusive neighbourhood.

"Let's go!" I bellowed, urging them to come with me to the French windows and escape. I'd seen what was going to happen next. But they just stood there, gaping. It was too late anyway. There was the sound of windows smashing, of wood bowing inwards. Nat's dad was rammed backwards by two or three of the intruders, as they flooded into the room from the hall and the kitchen.

Then they were at the French windows, piling in. A pincer movement, to catch all of us and make sure there was no getting away.

Nat's mother was the first to be savaged, and in spite of what I thought of her I took no great pleasure in what I saw. Teeth sinking into her neck, so that her head was virtually hanging off. Blood jetted upwards out of the stump like a geyser.

Nat was screaming as Tim swung his bat – hitting a couple of his attackers, but only knocking them back momentarily. He was covered in them seconds later, as they tore into his stomach, pulling out intestines right in front of my eyes, the light in Nat's hand illuminating a stark scene of bloodshed.

Nat's father was already being ripped limb from limb, the bottles of wine in his hand smashing as he squeezed them tight in his death throes. Then it was Nat's turn, as more ferals surged into the room through the smashed French windows. They swarmed over everything like oversized ants, and I moved forward to try and help. Tim had been her best bet, but her knight in shining armour was currently having his guts eaten somewhere on the floor. My way was blocked by this tide, and I could only gaze across at Nat, her petrified face picked out by her torch, drowning in that same sea as the woman I'd encountered back there on the road.

I stood facing the wall of bodies, some just as ravaged as their victims. Eyeballs hanging from sockets, ribs exposed in certain cases. I stared at them, understanding that at any moment they'd launch at me, drag me to the ground and start chomping on my flesh.

I'm not a stupid person; I'd worked out what

they were by now. What they *had* to be. Things that we'd been writing about, making movies about, for decades. Now here they were, large as life... as *death*, right in front of me and ready to feast. But they didn't. The ones facing me just turned and got down to join the others, searching for scraps that might be left over – from the couple who owned this house, from Tim. I tried not to think about Nat, it made me feel ill.

Instead I got out of there, while I still could. I went back through those French windows, to the end of the back garden, stepping over the broken fence there and out into the world.

And what a world it was: a changed world. A New World to reflect the New Year we now had. A world without Nat (she *had* been there with Tim, I reminded myself, but that was probably more of her parents' doing than hers). A world that didn't make sense to me anymore. So many questions...

Why had I been spared back at the house? Why hadn't I been eaten? Why hadn't Nat and the rest of them just come with me and fled when I begged them to? Why hadn't they understood what I'd been saying?

Why was I so hungry?

I hadn't really noticed before, but yes – I was ravenous. By the time I'd made it several blocks, I was practically doubled up with cramps. I felt so... so empty inside. I needed *filling up* somehow. The questions could wait; I had to find something to eat, right that minute.

There was another home not far away, a bungalow this time with an open front door, so I headed for that. Again there were no lights on inside; it was only now occurring to me that I hadn't seen any streetlamps working for a long while – I hadn't even noticed – so maybe the electricity had gone off? It had been on before though, because Nat and her family had obviously been watching the news, had seen enough to hide away from it... until I came along.

"It's one of them, from the news!"

Putting everything else out of my mind – I had to, all I could focus on was getting food – I wandered across and in through the front door. I didn't bother announcing my presence, what was the point? The people who owned the bungalow didn't know me. They'd attack either way. Nat and her clan had, after all.

I didn't give a shit anymore, I'd cross that

bridge when I came to it. But it was really dark inside the bungalow, much darker than it had been back at The Manor. I tried flicking the light switch and was rewarded with an answer about the electricity. It was definitely out. Feeling my way along inside the house, I soon found the kitchen – and, after rummaging around inside a few cupboards, I found a box of matches too. I could start my search for food, which I did in the upright fridge – a pool of water gathering at its base where the ice inside was melting. I opened the door, half expecting that little light to still come on. When it didn't, I struck a match so I could see what was in there. Some vegetables that looked as if they'd been on the turn before the power cut, margarine, milk... all well in date. Ah, some cheese. I've always been a notorious cheese fiend. Nat used to get me what she called my "stinky cheeses" as a treat sometimes. I'd had some just the other week for Christmas, as it happened, and that thought again made me feel sad. The way Xmas had turned out, but more importantly what I'd lost at New Year's.

Another groan from my stomach, so I greedily scoffed down the cheddar. It couldn't make me feel any worse, could it?

Wrong. No sooner had I washed it down with the milk – dairy was very big in our household – than my stomach lurched and I brought it all back up again. I struck another match and looked at the date on the cheese, something I probably should have done before eating it. But it was fine, and the fridge couldn't have been off *that* long.

I spotted some bread on the side and buttered that instead, scoffing it down. The same thing happened; I found myself bent over, spewing it all back up again. It was while I was on the floor that the bottom section – the freezer section – of the fridge started making noises. A tapping at first, then out and out banging.

I looked up and sideways, confused. Something was in there. Something that had got trapped? I remembered an old sitcom where a cat had snuck in and frozen to death inside one of those things. Looks like whatever was in there was lucky there *hadn't* been any electricity. It had probably saved its life.

I reached up and opened the door. There was something moving around in one of the see-through drawer compartments. Then a hand – fingers spread – pressed itself up against the clear surface. I started, yanking my head back. The match went out. How could there be a hand in there? Was the rest of the body inside, or just that appendage? I was thinking about those limbs I'd already seen moving around on their own...

I made to light another match, then realised I could still see; maybe even better than before. But that was soon forgotten when I realised my mistake. Those weren't fingers at all, but bloated worms of some kind. Tentatively, I reached out for the drawer, ready to pull my hand back instantly if there was any kind of danger. I tugged it open and immediately the worms crawled out, flopping onto the kitchen floor where they began to crawl slowly, arching their backs with each movement so that they looked more like caterpillars. They weren't those either, though.

They were sausages. Raw, defrosted sausages that had broken out of their packs.

I watched, open-mouthed, as they made their bid for freedom — these mish-mashes of meat. Something slammed against another one of the drawers, pushing it outwards on its own. I scrambled back out of the way, just in time to see a whole headless chicken climb up, using its wings to gain purchase and then hauling itself over the drawer's edge, like a soldier on an assault course climbing net. This was some kind of nightmare, had to be. I could accept – sort of – what had happened so far, but not this. This was too much.

Clutching my aching stomach, I got to my feet and retreated into an adjacent room, possibly the dining room. There was a loud squawk in my ear, and I jumped a final time, looking across to see a bird flapping about in a cage. Whoever had owned this place had left in such a hurry they hadn't bothered with their pet. It was some kind of parrot, and the closer I drew the more it bit at the metal bars, trying to break free.

Dead things liberated; living things trapped.

Then more pain in my gut, swiftly followed by a jabbing headache, as if someone was sticking an ice-pick in my ear. Everything went blurry. I wobbled, feeling myself pitching forward, but unable to do anything about it. I fell headlong into the dining table, collapsing it.

And for the second time that night, I blacked out.

~

I dreamed... or I think I did. I haven't dreamt since that night, so I can't be a hundred percent sure. It might even have been some strange out of body experience. Anyway, I dreamed that it was daytime, and I was walking through the streets again, but I was a ghost. And I wasn't alone. There were lots of us, all drifting – passing through cars, buildings, living people. I floated through the red car that had hit me, still wrapped around the lamppost.

I looked down at myself, my see-through body; thick, brown-blue veins were running up and down my arms, undulating, scratching at the surface. I drifted along, past Nat's parents' place, through all of them – Nat, her folks, Tim – when they came outside. They were waving at me to stop, but I just passed right through them, not looking back.

The streets didn't appear familiar to me, but I realised this was the route I must have taken to get to the bungalow, because there it was with its open doorway. I broke away from the pack, wafting sideways and through the entrance.

Drifting into the kitchen, where I saw the mess

on the floor – the water and the trails the reanimated meat had caused, climbing again, up and out of an open window. I sailed sideways, past the bird cage, and saw myself lying on the collapsed table. I stepped into my body and suddenly I was solid again, but I was also starving.

The thought of the dead flesh from the freezer made me feel even worse, however. Then I spotted the bird. The parrot still squawking to get out. I walked over and opened the cage door. I thought I was going to free it, but suddenly my arm and hand was out, grabbing the parrot, ignoring its thrashings. I opened my mouth and bit into the creature, ripping off its head and relishing the warm wetness of its blood on my lips, the living flesh as I swallowed it down.

I went to take another bite and—

—snapped awake, still on the table where I'd fallen, though in a slightly different position. *Might have just moved around on there, restless*, I thought to myself. More excuses, more ignoring the truth. Which is why I couldn't look at the empty birdcage as I rose and left the room, couldn't acknowledge the redness or scattered feathers, or the fact my stomach had stopped complaining. For now.

It was light out, so it must have been the following morning – unless I'd been there a day or more? I did what I automatically do – did – when I wake up and headed for the bathroom. But it was strange. No matter how long I stood there, I couldn't pee. I couldn't remember *wanting* to pee either, not since the pub on New Year's Eve. Same went for the other...

I gave up and went to the sink, splashing water on my face and looking in the mirror. At my grey face, the eyes sunken and dark. There were lumps sticking out of my neck where the bones looked like they were about to poke through. I touched them, and felt myself shiver.

No... no, I thought. I even shook my head, but had to turn away when I saw the grinding effect that had beneath the surface. *Why don't you take a look at your legs, as well? Go on, just drop your trousers and have a look what state* they're *in!*

(Okay, okay, so it took me a while to catch on – others were a lot faster. Yes, yes, I'm talking about you. Now stop trying to tickle me, you know I can't even feel it... I'll get to you in a little while. Let me tell them the rest first. Right, where was I? Oh yeah, I guess I knew but didn't

- 84 -

want to know, I'm sure that makes sense to a lot of you out there...)

I left the bathroom in a hurry and found myself wandering into the kitchen again. There was one way to prove it. One sure-fire way. I grabbed the handle of one of the kitchen knives in the rack, pressing the blade to my flesh. Just one cut, one movement with the knife and I'd know for sure. Wouldn't be able to deny it any longer.

I was just about to draw the stainless steel across my wrist when I heard the commotion outside.

Not again! I made my way to a window so I could look out. Up the road I saw another scene very similar the one I'd encountered after my accident, except here was a young man being chased, crying out for help. His pursuers weren't as many in number, say about fifteen or so, but they *were* armed and shouting – all threats, pretty much. I could see lengths of wood with nails hammered into them, axes, and what looked like sharp iron pokers being swung. One person threw a rock at the youth, who stumbled forward, but caught his balance just in time.

And I thought the same thing: *Not again!*

I wasn't going to let this happen *again*, especially not to a lad who could easily have been a student of mine. He looked pretty well built, the closer he came, but he was also outnumbered and unarmed.

I didn't like those odds, so I decided to change them. Now, I'm not Tim – he would probably have gone crashing in there, whacking people left, right and centre with his cricket bat. I'd always had it drummed into me:

Use your brains, David. Use your brains...

So I did. Tucking the knife away in my belt, under my coat, I went to the kitchen. Quickly searching through the cupboards, I found the ingredients I needed. I emptied any glass bottles I could find, and began mixing the liquids I'd dug out into those bottles. Some of it ran out down the sides, but that didn't matter – I was working against the clock, and that youth didn't have much longer left.

Nat's father had given me the idea with the bottles he was going to throw at me, but the contents of mine were a little more deadly than your average Merlot. Put it this way, if you know what you're doing you can really cook up a nice little surprise using ordinary household products – bleach with toilet cleaner, or bleach and vinegar... or all three. The kind of products Nat would probably have come up with a nice slogan for back in the day.

Nat...

I gritted my teeth, held my breath (yeah, I know now – why bother?) and mixed up a concoction in a couple of empty milk bottles. Then I hurried to the front door. I only just made it: the lad had already gone past and the gang were just about to. Before any of them could see me or do anything, I hurled one bottle, then the other. The first smashed in front of them, the second in the middle – right next to their feet.

No explosions, if that's what you're thinking. Just fumes. Strong ones, toxic ones. Enough to knock out an elephant. We were outside, but it was a fairly dull day without any wind, so the effect was pretty good. One by one the youth's attackers dropped, coughing and spluttering, flailing out at whatever was in front of them – even if it was one of their own. One man even impaled the person beside him with the poker he was holding.

Then they were on the concrete, lying there, completely unconscious.

The youth looked across at me. I could see now that he was wearing a tattered green jumper and jeans. His hair was blond, but it had lost its life, its vitality. In fact *he* looked muted, as if someone had turned down the contrast on a TV. From the colour of his skin, which I had to say matched mine, to his clothes: all were faded. He looked down at the people on the ground, then back up again at me, and raised a hand.

I approached, cautiously. Not at all sure I'd done the right thing here. This didn't feel like after the accident. That had felt *completely* right, trying to save the woman.

"Thanks!" he called out as I drew nearer. "Appreciated."

I nodded.

"I'm Sam. Who're you?"

I opened my mouth to speak, but nothing came out. Maybe I thought Sam wouldn't be able to understand, but deep down I knew from the second I lay eyes on him he would.

"It's okay, you got 'em good. That was... clever."

That was me all over, though. *So* clever.

"You're smart," he added, to bolster the compliment.

I nodded again.

"You hungry?" he asked.

And suddenly I was, as soon as he'd said it. I was starving again. He nodded to the prone figures, holding his hand out like Drake after laying down his cloak for the Queen. I frowned.

"You can go first," he explained. "If you like."

Go? I still didn't get it, even then. I shook my head anyway, ignoring the cracking sound, and Sam shrugged. He got down on his knees in front of the man who'd been stabbed with the poker, and took hold of his arm, rolling up the sleeve. Before I had a chance to grasp what he was doing, he'd already bitten into the flesh of the wrist. As out of it as he was, the man shrieked and began to sit up, but Sam pushed him back down and began gnawing on his throat, to silence – and finally finish – him. I stepped forward and grabbed Sam's shoulder, yanking him away.

"What the hell do you think you're doing?"

Sam gaped at me, before shrugging. "Er... I'm eating." I blinked; he *could* understand what I was saying. "You should try some, it's good. Guy was on his way out anyway."

A nonsense rhyme flashed through my head

from my childhood, about someone with Sam's name who liked to eat green eggs and ham. No he bloody well didn't! What this Sam ate was much, much worse.

"Fuck." The word didn't seem strong enough somehow, and didn't seem proper seeing as I could now apparently communicate. This was my first real conversation since the accident. But then what was *proper* about any of this? I don't know what I thought I was expecting. If Sam had contracted this cannibal thing, then wouldn't he be like those crazies who'd been after the girl? Like those who had broken into The Manor and taken Tim, Nat's parents...

Nat.

Even so, the end result was the same. What Sam was doing to the people I'd brought down... No, this wasn't right at all.

"What's the matter? You squeamish? You soon get over that when the cramps start. Look..." He held up a piece of flesh he'd torn from the man's neck. "Here, take it. Tastes just like chicken."

Or parrot? I couldn't help a small internal giggle at that, but this wasn't funny. This *so* wasn't funny. Sam was killing this guy. *Had* killed him, in fact, judging by the fact the bubbles that had been coming from his wrecked airway had now stopped. Had killed him and was eating him. I let those words settle in my mind. Then I shook my head again.

Sam shrugged, then popped the morsel in his mouth. "Of course, the really good stuff is inside there." He pointed to the skull. Oh, there was no denying *anything* now. No denying what Sam was at all. And no denying what I must surely be, for him to be able to understand me, for us to be talking at all. It explained everything: what had happened during my accident – a broken neck, cutting off the air supply (in a marginally more pleasant way than the guy who'd just fallen prey to Sam), crippled but still walking; what had happened when I'd been passed over at Nat's parents' – I wasn't *fresh* enough; why the food from the fridge hadn't done anything to help with my hunger, hadn't even stayed in my system long enough – because it was the wrong kind. Because my system, such as it was, didn't work that way anymore. Was this to be my diet now, what Sam was dining on?

No, I wouldn't have it.

"That's delicious, what's in his head. Like creamed rice or something, man."

I thought I was going to throw up. Except I knew I wasn't. I'd only done that when I'd tried to go against the natural order of things. *Natural?* How could any of this be natural?

I grabbed him again and tried to pull him back, but he was bigger than me. Stronger. He shrugged off my hand and rose, facing me, and I saw a little of the animal in him then as his lip curled. I'd interrupted his feast, refused to share in it even. Could there be any more of a social faux pas for our kind?

I didn't give a toss. I pulled the knife still in my belt and waved it in front of him. Sam stopped snarling, and laughed. Then he walked forward and allowed the blade to penetrate his chest. I pulled a face, pushing him backwards off my weapon and staring at it, then at Sam.

There was no blood on it, nor at Sam's wound – just an odd-coloured slime, dripping. It was dark and might have been blood once, before New Year's Day, but wasn't anything of the sort now.

Your heart bleeds, right? Maybe even literally.

"You're having trouble, I get that," said Sam. "Trust me, it's cool. But you're going to have to wise up sooner or later." He nodded down at the body beneath him. "Pick a side, y'know?"

But I'd already started, hadn't I? I'd defended Sam against these people, *saved* him from them (although I did wonder what they could even have done to him... but we'll get to that in a moment). There was just one thing left before my initiation was complete.

"And I owe you for this, so if you want to travel together that's okay by me. But my mum always told me when I was growing up: never let good food go to waste."

I waved a hand, then made my way back to the bungalow. I couldn't be a witness to this. Not yet. Not on such a scale. I could still see that woman and what had been done to her. I could still see Nat. So I waited on the couch, my stomach growling.

When he was done, or had eaten as much as he could, Sam strolled over to the bungalow. He sat down in the armchair opposite me.

"Hope you're pleased with yourself," I said, a look of disgust still on my face.

He gave a half smile. "Well, I'm full – so that's something. It's a feeling I'm still getting used to." When he saw my puzzled expression, he explained: "Oh, I live – *lived* – on the streets." It's where Sam died, on those streets, from exposure and hunger. It made me feel a little different about what he'd just done. Sam had been fading long before he turned. "People are – *were* – great at Christmas, going round with parcels for the needy and such. Most years anyway. But it all seems to tail off afterwards, and then it's worse than ever." He'd seen the whole thing from the front ranks, experienced it as it happened: the change. Was probably one of the very few who had. "But don't ask me how it happened, or why," he continued, "because that's beyond me."

It's beyond us all. Still. But I have my theories same as everyone else.

Sam had been with another two or three like him – like us – when those hunters had come upon them. They'd taken down his friends and were about to do the same with him.

"But they can't kill you," I pointed out. "You're already dead." Not even cutting pieces off did anything.

"They've tried burning us," Sam explained, leaning back. "That didn't work either." And he went on to tell me about the figures of ash he'd seen, those burnt by flamethrowers or blown up, and those who'd risen up out of the crematoriums.

Risen.

I had no idea about the range until I met Sam, that there were those that could be mistaken for alive and, at the other end of the scale, those whose flesh had rotted from their bones decades – or even centuries – ago. "But the living have gotten creative. Realised that if they cut us up small enough with chainsaws, with axes like they had back there, then lock the bits away –"

"Lock them away where?"

"Anywhere they can find: rooms, containers..."

I thought about the sausage and the chicken, clambering to get out. It must be like a living hell, bits of you shut away in different places, not whole anymore and no chance of ever being again. That's the fate Sam's friends had suffered. It was the fate I'd saved him from. A cruel fate.

I sat, silent for a moment or two, then said, "You mentioned travelling, back there. That I could go with you."

Sam nodded. "Like I said, I owe you."

"But where to?"

That's when he told me, about the place he

was heading for. About where he and his friends were headed until they ran into the hunters. "There are rumours going around about a gathering. That those like us are coming together in larger numbers."

I laughed. "You mean like a promised land or something?"

"No, not really. Just somewhere safe, I guess."

"And where might that be?"

Sam smiled. "Where else?"

Yes, it was a graveyard. But the biggest one in the county, maybe even beyond that. It would take a few weeks to reach it, though we picked up quite a few stragglers along the way: Ken the former window cleaner, for example; Maggie, who'd worked in a solicitors' office before all this happened; kids Stephen and Lindsay, no more than nine or ten years old (the first living people they'd eaten were the men who'd abducted, tortured and murdered them); bricklayer Phil; ex-post woman Nancy... the list went on and on. All were in various states of decomposition, and two – a married couple called Lillian and Sid – had reconstructed themselves from their own ashes, to find each other again in death. Not all members of our group were of the same intelligence level, though.

I soon learned that some of the risen – that's the name I gave to them, and those still alive were unrisen, obviously – were as feral as they appeared. Like those who'd chased the woman or attacked The Manor. Some simply had trouble thinking, a bit like it had been in the life before. Sorry, couldn't resist that: but it's true.

We also came across a fair few unrisen hunters, and had a number of close calls. One of which was turned around by Frankie. I haven't told you about Frankie yet, have I? Who leapt up and took down a guy wielding an industrial strimmer – which would have made a hell of a mess out of myself and several members of our group. A black and grey blur leaping through the air, teeth clamping down on strimmer-man's forearm. Tugging him to the ground, then savaging the guy.

He came over to me afterwards and started wagging his tail. Can you believe it? Yes, that's right – Frankie's a dog. A deceased lurcher who somehow found us and joined our group, and certainly proved his worth on that occasion (I named him after Frankenstein, because he's got all these stitches all over him; probably where a vet had tried – and failed – to save him from whatever had been wrong). He was also pretty good at sniffing out the unrisen and warning us about them in advance... not that our own skills in that department hadn't improved, too. All our senses were keener now, in fact. Better.

I still hadn't touched human flesh, let alone what was inside the head. I left those 'delights' to the others in our group, while I contented myself with any living animals I could get my hands on. I figured, I'd eaten chicken, fish, beef while I'd still been alive – why did that have to change? Of course it had to be still living, because I couldn't stomach dead meat now. Something about our 'metabolism' can't handle that. I'm looking into why. I've looked into a lot of things in my time here. But I'm getting off topic again.

Back to our journey.

It didn't take us as long as I thought to reach that cemetery, though. Mainly because we don't have to sleep. Another way in which we're superior to the unrisen, I suppose. To begin with I kept wanting to stop and rest, but I soon realised I was only doing this out of habit, pure and simple. I didn't actually need to. Sam thought it was amusing, and teased me so much that I shook myself out of it. We can also see quite well in the dark, which made it easier to travel at night-time.

I'll tell you all about that journey one day, but right now it's not important. This is.

Finally, we made it, cresting a hill and spotting those huge iron gates in the distance. The cemetery itself, on the outskirts of a city two or three over from mine, was surrounded by a wall, adjacent to a church, and backed out onto woodland beyond. "We're here," Sam announced proudly. It had been his idea to come, after all. As we made our way to the entrance, however, we began to think it had all been a huge waste of time. The place looked deserted. If there had been any of our kind here, then surely they'd moved on long ago. I thought Sam was going to cry... not that he could. None of us can, if you've noticed. We feel like it sometimes, and our faces screw up, but nothing comes out. The well has dried up, our tear ducts barren.

Anyway, Sam needn't have worried. As we attempted to force the gate open, several figures appeared out of nowhere. "Who are you?" asked the closest, a fellow who looked like he'd been in the ground for a few years – clothes and skin as bad as each other. It was one of the reasons we didn't smell them, because they smelt like us. Of decay.

"We're here to join..." I didn't know what to call it really: a family; a sect; a cabal? As it turned out that was enough information and they opened the gates *for* us. The man who'd asked who we were turned and looked at a skeletal form on his right, then addressed it... him (I discovered later that the skeleton was called Newton, and he'd once been a servant to the monarchy back at the turn of the last century). "Take them to see Reynolds," he instructed.

We were led through the 'yard, and saw that the risen here had appeared from out of tombs and vaults, from holes in the ground where the dead had clawed their way up to see the light of day once more. Now, it seemed, they were defensive hiding positions.

We found Reynolds, their leader, camped out in the largest of the vaults – an elaborate structure that must have been home to some kind of nobility once, though they'd apparently left this place after the New Year reinvigorated them. The interior was lit with torches on the walls, which burned away. For effect only.

He sat on a large chair inside, which had clearly been brought here for him. It had to be large, because *he* was large. Massive, in fact. He looked for all the world like one of those wrestlers from America, the ones that sweat a lot and could lift you off the ground with a single hand.

Reynolds was recently dead, and only looked about as grey as myself or Sam – with a lethal-looking scar running from his temple, down a cheek, and across his jawline. I froze when I saw him, but then I noticed the other figure sitting quietly not far away in the corner. A woman – Reynolds' woman? – also freshly dead, about my age; she had dark hair and her eyes caught mine, just for a moment. There was an unusual warmth there. Before I knew what was happening, or could stop it, Sam was approaching the behemoth. In fact he went right up to him and said, "We've come to be part of—" Like me, Sam never got the word out, either; because Reynolds rose up in one swift movement, making my friend look small by comparison. The man's hand was out in seconds, sweeping backwards and lifting Sam off his feet. The youth flew across the length of that stone room, landing awkwardly on the far side. I looked from Sam back to Reynolds, and then at the woman, whose hand had gone to her mouth. She looked as if she was about to rise, go to Sam, but thought better of it.

"You speak when spoken to in here, boy!" boomed Reynolds, the words echoing off the walls and making them sound even louder in my ears. You didn't need to have been an anthropologist to work out how he'd taken over as leader, and why people obeyed his commands. He was the strongest of them here, maybe even the strongest of us all. Certainly of the risen we'd encountered so far.

Behind me Frankie was growling, but I turned and put a hand on his head to calm him.

I found my voice then, finally, keeping my distance from Reynolds, though. "We're sorry," I began, my voice cracking and my eyes flicking over to the woman again briefly. "Sam meant no disrespect. He's just... excited to be here. He's the one who *brought* us here. We wish only to be counted amongst your number." The words sounded stupid, even as I was saying them – like

I was in some kind of Shakespeare play. Reynolds' eyes narrowed and he 'breathed' in and out quickly (I say breathed, but that too – the familiar in and out of the chest – was just a habit carried over from life. No heartbeat, no need for oxygen. Oh, the explorations we could undertake someday... of the ocean, of outer space... real life SF dramas!... and never any need for cumbersome diving-gear or spacesuits).

Sam was clambering to his feet, shaking his head. He wasn't hurt physically, couldn't be, but his pride was. I could see it on his face. Thankfully it was a look too subtle for Reynolds to notice.

The big man continued to regard me coolly. Then, voice lowering a little, though not much, he said "And what makes you think we *want* you?" He glanced across at the woman and grinned. She remained tight-lipped.

Want us? What was he talking about? According to Sam this was where we should be, where all of us needed to be? A safe place. But if it was a promised land then it looked like those promises were turning out to be worthless.

"I..." My mind went blank. I hadn't been expecting that reaction, I have to say. When I could see Reynolds losing interest, I heard my parents' voice in my head again:

Use your brains, David.

I quickly blurted out, "Your defences could use a little shoring up for starters."

Reynolds glared at me. "*What?*"

"What if the unrisen—"

"The what?" Reynolds interrupted.

"It... it's what he calls the humans," Sam told him.

I nodded. "What if they decide to storm those gates, crash through them with a vehicle of some sort? All your people are on the inside, and it'd be too late by then."

Reynolds rubbed his chin, and the woman finally spoke, standing and placing a hand on his arm. "I think we should hear what he has to say. Remember the 'incident' I told you about before you arrived." I found out later this was a skirmish between the unrisen and the risen out in the graveyard itself, involving the young woman, almost resulting in the whole place being set on fire. Superior numbers had won the day, but only just.

"*I* put those defences in place," Reynolds said, annoyed, "*because* of what you told me."

"I-I know," said the woman, eyes flicking over at me. The look didn't go unnoticed this time. She let her hand fall from his arm.

"You really should listen to him," Sam broke in at that point. "He's smart. He saved me from a gang of them when we first met, did something with some chemicals. Put them all out for the count."

"You some kind of egghead, eh?" Reynolds sneered. I could see what he thought of that. I was probably his least favourite kind of person. We'd get along like oil and water.

"I wouldn't say that. But I know a little bit about this and that."

Reynolds looked back at the woman one final time, and sighed. "All right, tell us what kind of fancy defences you have in mind and we'll see."

It was a gamble. For all I knew he might just want to pick those brains I'd been using and then turf us all out again. But I told him anyway, and to his credit he listened intently. When I'd finished, he nodded.

"All right, good," he said. "That might work."

"I think it's a great idea," offered the woman.

"I said *all right*," Reynolds snapped, rounding on her. She shrank back. He ordered Newton to take us out again, and he did so – but then took it upon himself to show us around the place, give us the guided tour.

"How long has Reynolds been in charge?" I asked as we navigated the headstones.

"Not as long as he likes to think, sir," croaked Newton, through vocal chords that were barely even there. *And too long for some*, I thought.

It seemed as if all the inhabitants had surfaced now to see who these newcomers were, and by the time we'd finished our circuit of the place there was quite a crowd gathering. The woman from the vault was present as well, bending to talk to Stephen and Lindsay. There were other kids present as well and she appeared to be introducing ours to them.

She looked up when we came over, shielding her eyes against the dying sun in the sky. "They're adorable," she said. "Yours?"

I shook my head. "Not that lucky, I'm afraid."

"They can join our school if they like, this week we're learning about—"

"You teach?" I shook my head and apologised for interrupting her. It was just that to find someone of the same profession out here... and still doing what they'd done in life.

"I know what you're thinking. What's the point? But there's *every* point. We might not be how we were before, but sometimes different can be a good thing. Sometimes it can make things better."

"Like Reynolds? Has he made things better here?"

She didn't answer, mainly because she'd spotted the 'man' himself emerging from the vault. But I'd get my chance to talk to her, properly and alone, soon enough.

"At least tell me your name," I said quickly, and in hushed tones.

"It's Helen," she said simply. "Helen Kirby."

~

You've met Helen before. Yes, you have. A little while ago, she was the one in here with me, trying to distract me. But she was just being playful, because that's who she *really* is. Funny and intelligent and sweet. It was who she was before, not that anybody had noticed it much back then.

That's probably why she committed suicide on New Year's Eve.

When we finally got a chance to chat, she told

me her story. It's a long one, so I won't repeat it now. Maybe some other time. (She might even tell it you herself.) But she'd gone through the same confusion, the same denial as me – journeying through her hometown, not knowing what was happening, not being able to make herself heard.

Helen ended up here and, in that fight with the unrisen she'd mentioned back in the vault, she'd finally realised who – and what – she was. Not only that, she'd embraced it. It's mainly Helen I discuss those theories with, about our species making a leap forward. She's maintained right from the start that it's a good thing, that we're the superior race now, that the unrisen – the *humans* – won't and can't last.

"The ones we beat thought they were the only people left. But they weren't. They aren't. There are others still out there, others who are dangerous." She makes a lot of sense, Helen.

"So what's with you and Reynolds?" I asked her the first chance I got. "Are you *with* him?"

"He wishes," she said sadly, eyes downcast. "And maybe he thinks that one day..." Helen let the sentence trail off, then looked up at me. "I thought I'd done with men like that when I died.

And along *he* came, just when we were starting to make some headway with this place. Starting to make it feel like a home. Now... well, now I don't really know what it is."

I got the opportunity to observe a little of how Reynolds operated in the coming weeks, the way he would send the most proficient scavengers out there to look for isolated unrisen, to capture and bring them back for food. Not for the camp, mainly for him – for Reynolds. Everyone else was left with the scraps he gave them, including Helen.

"You still haven't...?" she asked one night as she ate raw flesh out of a bowl.

I shook my head. "Just haven't developed a taste for it."

"You must be getting awful cramps."

"I'll survive," I told her. And I was doing. Getting by on whatever wild animals I could catch in traps that I set on the outskirts of the graveyard, in the undergrowth and woodland. If I could see the others were struggling, I'd share whatever I'd caught with them. Once I even brought back a deer that had wandered here from God knows where, and we all tucked in around a fire out in the open. Reminded me of those camping trips I used to go on in my teens, back in my own student days.

Helen encouraged me to try the other meat, told me that it's the way things worked now, that we're all part of the same system and every time we ate those who hadn't changed then we were becoming more whole as a species. That they'd understand in the end, the people being "absorbed".

But I just couldn't bring myself to do it.

"It tastes just like chicken, you know," she said to me.

"So I keep being told. And what's going to happen when we run out, when all the living people are gone? When we've become completely 'whole'? Is that when you're going to come round to my way of thinking?"

"Maybe someone will figure something out. Maybe even you, David."

"Call me Dave," I said with a laugh.

But my growing friendship with Helen was not going down well with our fearless leader. Whenever he summoned me for a meeting, usually to talk battle strategies like he was a general planning a war, he would warn me that she was off limits.

"She's not a piece of property," I made the mistake of informing him once, when I thought I was safe. When I thought he was relying on me to the point where he wouldn't do anything.

He'd come at me then, lifting me and slamming me against the wall of the vault. "How *dare* you speak to me like that!"

Fortunately, fate chose that moment to bear out what I'd said about the defences. First Frankie's frenzied barking, alerting us to the presence of unrisen. Then, as they approached, Lillian and Sid, plus a few more of the ash-risen who'd arrived since we got here, stirred, sweeping up out of the ground on the outside of the gates – where they were dug in much better than any of the others ever could be – and coalescing. They got into eyes, mouths, the inside of cars, leaving the confused and disorientated hunters for the rest of our clan to tackle.

It was all over by the time Reynolds and I got outside. And though he could see how effective my ideas had been, he still stormed off like a child having a tantrum.

This attack and a few others after that night made Reynolds keen to step up his offensive, to take the battle to the unrisen instead of continuing to build our defences on site. Except he wasn't the one going out and facing the danger half the time, and even when he did he would hang back and lead from the rear while his 'troops' – so terrified of him they'd do anything – would be sent in ahead.

"Don't you understand, you're actually drawing more attention *to* us," I told him during one of those meetings, but he waved a hand dismissively. "Look, have you given any more thought to my sleeper agent idea. There are risen that look almost human, can pretty much *pass* for human if they keep their mouths shut. We can infiltrate some of their hideouts. At least find out what some of the unrisen are—"

"Stop calling them that!" Reynolds boomed again. "Those are your names, not mine! Go away now, I don't want to hear this."

He didn't want to hear anything, in fact. And whereas before he did at least ask advice, listen to strategies – given against my better judgement – he thought he knew better. He got careless. And it was this that ended up costing many of his complement... not their lives, because they had none to lose, but the closest thing to it they possessed.

A simple trap, with simple bait: a handful of armed unrisen, fleeing from Reynolds and his troops. Only for our kind to turn a corner and come face to face with a combine harvester, which was suddenly gunned up and used to rip them to shreds. The pieces had no doubt been gathered up then and disposed of in the way Sam had described the first time we encountered each other.

Far from demoralising the unrisen, picking them off, Reynolds was actually firing them up. Forcing them to band together, to come up with strategies of their own.

Two of those involved with the harvester debacle were Phil and Maggie. Phil and Maggie who'd come with us on our journey, who thought they were heading somewhere better with us. Where they'd be safe. Not to be used as pawns in some lunatic's war games.

"The stupid, stupid bastard," I said to Sam when we heard the news, Reynolds and his decimated numbers returning.

"This can't go on, Dave," he said, and I could see how much more muted he'd become since we got here.

"It shouldn't have gone on this long," I told him. "I know that now."

"But what can we do?"

"There's only one thing we *can* do. What I should have done some time ago. Challenge Reynolds for the leadership of this place."

"You're kidding. He'd bury you."

I raised an eyebrow at his choice of words, considering where we were. And I knew I couldn't win against brute force like that – it was how Reynolds had maintained control for so long in the first place.

No, I had other plans.

I heard my folks again: *Brains can win over brawn, so use your brains, David.*

Use your brains.

~

When I called Reynolds out, I did it publicly.

I got Sam and Newton to gather everyone they could, and form a semi-circle outside the vault. "H-Hey Reynolds!" I shouted. For someone who'd never really been in a fight in his life, let alone won one, I thought I was doing all right. "Reynolds, get out here you piece of shit!"

Doing all right that is, until the giant of a man came outside, stooping to clear the entrance. "What do *you* want?"

He looked bigger than ever, if that were possible. I swallowed dryly; there was actually no other way *for* me to swallow.

"We have to talk."

"Oh?" he roared.

Helen appeared from behind him, a concerned look on her face. I hadn't told her what I'd decided to do. I couldn't, not until I knew I could pull it off. "Dave, what are you doing?"

"What I have to. What he's left me no choice but to do." I nodded to the crowds gathered. "I think everyone around here's had just about enough of you and the way you're doing things."

Reynolds sneered. "Is that a fact?"

"It is. T-They're all just too scared to say anything."

He strode forwards, within metres of me now. I could hear Frankie barking in the distance somewhere. Helen put herself between Reynolds and me. "Please," she said, looking first to him, then back in my direction. "Please stop."

"Helen... Helen, let him pass."

She looked at me with pleading eyes, and it was then I knew that our friendship had become much more than that over our long talks, getting to know each other (much longer talks than I'd shared with Nat when we first met). Then Reynolds snorted and made to proceed. Helen reached out to hold him back – a gesture only, because she could do nothing to stop him; no more than Phil or Maggie against that damned harvester. And he brushed her off easily, swept her aside with an arc of his large arm. She tripped and fell on the path, the gravel scraping her legs.

It was my turn to snarl, taking a step towards Reynolds before hesitating.

"Well, come on then – what are you waiting for, *egghead*?"

When I showed no signs of covering the remaining distance, Reynolds set off after me. Except he stopped at the last minute, gaping. Next he froze up *completely*, unable to take another step. An effect of the surprise I'd slipped into his most recent meal. I was nervous: not because I was facing him, but because I was worried I hadn't timed all this exactly right. In fact, I could have done with it kicking in before he attacked Helen, but...

A toxin. A very special creation of mine, using

drugs smuggled in by the scavengers I'd befriended – including new recruit, ex-postwoman Nancy. Culled from pharmacies and doctors' surgeries, I mixed up a batch of my own special concoction, which had to work from the stomach, in lieu of any circulatory system. You see, we still sort of *digest* food, it... fills us up, if you like, and that's what I was banking on. We work differently to the risen, we work *better*. Our bodies use it, absorb it, even if it's been poisoned. Ah, poison – the chosen weapon the get rid of unwanted dictators and monarchs for generations.

I'd used my brains... or, more accurately, I used someone else's. The person who Reynolds had dined on last. Devouring that delicacy Sam had sung the praises of. A delicacy I'd already tainted.

Now I approached, leaning in close to his ear so I could whisper: "*That's* what I was waiting for."

I took out the knife from my belt, where I still kept it hidden under my coat. Had done ever since I'd first picked it up. I traced the scar down Reynolds face, conscious that everyone was watching me. That Helen was watching me. It was time to get on with this, but first I had some unfinished business to attend to.

"Want to know a secret?" I whispered. "I know how you got that scar. I've known for a little while now. Where you were on New Year's Eve. What you did." You see, I never forget a face; it just takes me a while to place it sometimes. To remember. Especially as the last time I saw it I was flying over the bonnet of a car. I opened up that scar again now, but instead of the blood that had dripped from it – the blood I'd followed, as the head-wound slowly killed Reynolds somewhere – that dark-coloured slime leaked out. The stuff that actually helps us take in food. He'd heard the rumours, same as everyone else; decided to come here. Decided he wanted to take it over.

I stabbed him, repeatedly and in a frenzy. It was his fault I was like this; Reynolds had done this to me. I stabbed even as he toppled over: stabbed, slashed and cut. I didn't even notice Frankie joining me, to help where he could with his teeth. I worked on Reynolds until there were only pieces left, the littlest pieces imaginable – as small as those bits gathered after the harvester had done its worst.

I'd gather Reynolds up afterwards as well. Do the same to him as the unrisen had done to our kind. Contain him. Each bit in a separate place, locked away. It was the only way to be sure. It's the only way with any of us to be sure. That's what makes us so dangerous.

That's what makes us *better*.

~

My story's nearly at an end now. Just a few more loose ends to tie up.

I took over in that graveyard, as you probably expected I might. My own little kingdom, I guess you'd call it. King David – that makes me laugh. It's biblical, just like the event that happened, or some people's interpretation of it at any rate (just who were the saved and who were the damned anyway? We were the ones living next to the church, after all). But if I rule then I do it fairly, and with the love of my people. Not through fear, like Reynolds did. Helen is by my side, of course: advisor and... Well, I don't really need to draw you a picture, I don't think. She's here right now again, in fact, as I bring this to a close.

More of our kind arrive at the 'yard day by

day, especially as word travels about the things happening here. The community feel. My mum and dad are even with me, supporting me, still telling me to use my brains. Helen never really knew hers and doesn't *want* to see them again (something for which I gave a small 'thank you'). One day all this will spread beyond our home. In fact, I'm making sure of it.

My experiments continue, you see – one of which is with sound. About the way we hear differently, the way we hear our language. As with our sight, that's better too, like I hinted at before. We can hear on levels that only animals like Frankie used to be able to.

The frequency I'm broadcasting on now, for example. After many days with volunteers, transmitting my voice across various distances, I managed to figure it out. It's something the unrisen might tap into one day; who knows, maybe they'll even figure out our tongue. But not yet, I hope. Unless there's someone like me on their side, that is (oh yes, I've chosen mine finally – what choice did I have? – and I suppose I really ought to thank Reynolds for what he did, though it pains me to do so.)

It's possible leaders of their own might be

emerging, with plans and schemes about how to defeat us. Reynolds didn't exactly do anything to help in that respect, prodding the hornet's nest.

But they should be warned, because I'm coming up with more and more surprises every day, ably assisted by Newton. And we've really built up the defences here, all under the capable supervision of my chief of security – or commander of the guards, whichever you prefer. Yes, it's Sam. Other dogs like Frankie have been found, too, providing us with more than enough warning should any attacks occur.

I don't want to fight, because that's not in my nature. But I will if I have to; you know that now. And I fight dirty. Any unrisen planning on continuing the war with us should think twice, should either run away as far as they can – if they can even find anywhere our kind haven't taken over – or join us. I'm not talking about volunteering to be eaten. There are other ways. The same way Helen became risen. It'll only hurt for a moment, and then you'll be better. So much better.

Just as I'm working on ways to stop the decay we're all experiencing – though some might say that's the natural order of things, as well – I'm also working on that problem about the meat I discussed with Helen. Even taking into consideration the fact I still don't... *partake*, the supply will run out one day. Maybe animals bred for that purpose, to be eaten raw, will be the solution. Maybe not; maybe I can come up with something even better. Something more appetising.

Something that also tastes like chicken?

Who knows, that's in the future. But what about that future? I think about it sometimes. We're all going to see it, the risen. We're going to exist for a long, long time. I wonder what kind of planet it will be in years to come. What we'll make of it, the dominant species on Earth.

It's my hope that we'll all become one big community, that we'll start again – without the mistakes of the past. Friendly links to the risen in other countries. Peace, finally.

But then I think of Reynolds and how many more like him there might be in our number. Even when all the humans are gone, will we still have to fight risen like him?

In any event, our exclusive little neighbourhood is a start. And that's why we're broadcasting today, why we've broken into this tower, why we've jimmy rigged the transmitter and powered it with a generator. To reach you, to invite you to come and join us. To get you to spread the word even wider.

Helen once said to me, "This is the time of the dead." Didn't you? She's nodding. And it is. It's our time. The chance of a new beginning. But it's also a reckoning. A time to stand up and be counted.

And, I think, if we're smart – if we're clever – then we can do things better this time around.

This is David... Dave Hawthorne...

Dead man, and proud of it...

...signing off.

Dead End

All good things must come to an end, isn't that what they say?

Some bad things, as well. That's what's happening here, things are coming to a head. One way or another, things are ending. It's been a long, hard-fought battle, but at last, at long last there's a winner.

My name is Carl Maxwell, I'm still alive, and this is how the end began.

~

You know the story by now, you'll all have your *own* stories no doubt. Well, this is mine. I was working on New Year's Eve, same as I had been all through the holidays, and in the run up to the festive period. They get paranoid at that time of year, you see. It's when homes have the most break-ins, and it's when shops do as well. That's where I come in... came in at any rate. I worked security at Crescent View Mall; not exactly the career I wanted for myself, but it was steady work and I was grateful for it, especially after that bitch of an ex-wife took me for all I was worth.

I always figured I'd go into the army, just like Dad did, maybe even reach command level someday, be in charge of my own squad of soldiers. But my trick knee put paid to that. I'd wanted to make up for what happened to him, to balance things out somehow. Make him proud.

Dad was killed in action when me and Sandra were only kids; things were never right after that, and me going into the army – in spite of what Mum said – would have been what he wanted. We had so many rows over that, Mum and me, and she was glad when I finally failed my medical. That caused a stinker of a fight. It's probably one of the reasons she hasn't spoken to me in years.

Sandra? Oh, she's my little sister. I was living with her when it all went down, kipping on her couch in fact. She's never had a serious relationship in her life, so she was glad of the company. We've always got on well, me and Sand. She was all I could think about after I left the mall, and...

Slow down Carl, you're skipping bits. Just wanting to get everything out quickly, I guess. Where was I? Oh yeah, the mall. So there I was, on my own – skeleton staff (no pun intended) during the holidays, which I know doesn't tally with the paranoia thing, but like everyone else during the recession they'd made major cuts around the place. There was even some talk of it closing down, if many more shops went tits up. As it turned out, it wasn't the recession that did for that place.

But, anyway, I was on my own.

I suppose they figured it only took one man to keep an eye on the CCTV, to patrol every once in a while, raise the alarm if something happened. I didn't mind working while everyone else partied. It was more money, and what reason did I have to celebrate anyway? Ordinarily, Sandra would have been out on the town, but she'd come down with flu – actually, I'd passed it on to her. I shrug stuff like that off, while she comes down with them like a ton of bricks. So we were both missing out... right?

I'd been having trouble sleeping in the daytime, mainly due to Sand coughing and sneezing; sound really carried in that small flat of hers. I don't mention this as an excuse – hell, I'm hardly going to get into trouble for this stuff now, am I; at the same time I'm also not proud of it – but as an explanation as to why I was asleep during the preamble to what happened next. I remember doing a patrol, then returning to the office, gazing at the banks of monitors there, feeling my eyelids grow heavier and heavier. I even slapped myself awake at one point, but it didn't seem to help.

The next thing I knew, I heard glass breaking. That woke me up, and I started, my legs falling off the table where I'd had them resting – professional, eh? My first thought was, you guessed it, someone was breaking into the place. I imagined trucks lined up or circling the mall, teams of robbers in black and white striped jumpers and masks like the one the Lone Ranger used to wear, helping themselves to goods from the shops. Then I remembered: the place had security bars anyway. Even if someone *had* broken a window, they couldn't get in. The most likely explanation was that late night revellers, more than a little worse for wear, had lobbed something at one of the storefronts on the veranda again.

That theory seemed even more likely when I switched to a few external cameras, as opposed to the ones that were just showing me the inside of the mall, the inside of the stores. I gasped when I saw how many of them there were, though. Instead of teams of robbers, there were dozens of drunks, hell-bent on getting into this building. For what reason, I had no idea. Times were hard, sure – but where I used to live, you didn't go around doing stuff like that. In the bigger cities, maybe. You saw the rioting on the news and tutted, safe in the knowledge that it hadn't reached your little corner of the world... yet. Perhaps tonight was the night? And here I was, trapped inside this place on my own.

I picked up the phone straight away to call for help, but couldn't get through to the emergency services. Couldn't get through to anyone, as it goes. Not even Sand was picking up at the flat – which worried me, I have to admit. I had my own, more immediate problems to deal with, however, and it was possible that my sister had simply drugged herself up to the eyeballs (you should see her medicine cabinet in the bathroom, like a pharmacy it is... was... shit). Still didn't explain why the authorities weren't answering, mind. I tried my mobile next, but that wasn't working at all. It was New Year's Eve, though... New Year's *Day*, actually, as I discovered when I glanced at the clock. The networks are always busy or crash on that particular night, don't they?

In the meantime, the numbers outside were increasing. Dozens were becoming tens of dozens right in front of my eyes, all trying to get inside somehow. There was no cavalry on its way, so I decided to go down there and try to reason with these people. As drunk as they so obviously were, maybe if they saw that I was just an ordinary Joe doing an ordinary job – about to lose that job if they kept this up – they might disperse? As long as I was on the other side of those safety bars, I was okay, surely?

I left the office, headed down in the lift to the ground floor. My boots squeaked on the floor as I made my way down to the main entrance. And if what I'd seen on the monitors was bad, then it was much worse up close and personal. The crowds were starting to resemble something at an out-of-control football match, except I was the only one on the opposing team's side.

I could also see what had caused the noises I'd heard: some of the people had stuck their heads and arms through the security bars and banged on the glass frontage until it had cracked in certain spots, smashed in others. One man had punched through the glass, his fist still there in the hole, and he raked it backwards and forwards, the flesh being sawn off in clumps.

"Fucking hell..." I whispered under my breath. What were these people on? It was more than just drink, had to be. What then? Some kind of mass drug taking, hallucinatory drugs at that? They certainly didn't seem to be feeling pain – *any* of them.

I'd been so busy looking at the damage, at the clumps of them massing, I hadn't really taken in any of their features. But now I was close enough, I began to look properly at them. There was something very *wrong* about some of those folk – not all, granted, some looked perfectly normal apart from a sort of vacant look on their faces. Others, though, were... I don't know how else to describe it, other than diseased. Or at least that's how they appeared to me. I'd soon learn that they were in fact decomposed; *decomposing* more accurately. Their skin was grey, eyes bulged in hollow sockets, teeth were abnormally large, jutting out through thinning lips. But a few, my God, a few of them were virtually skeletal in nature. Like they hadn't had a decent meal in weeks, maybe months. Remember when there was all that footage on the TV of the starving masses in the third world, back in the 80s? Feed the world and all that? This was much, much worse. As I studied the mob more closely, I saw insects crawling across clothing, worms dangling from wrists. Maggots falling like confetti from a bride and groom after a wedding, shaken loose by their movements.

I looked from them to the inside of the mall. There was something very familiar about all this, but I couldn't quite place it.

But I didn't have any more time to think about that, because the bars were buckling, actually giving way under the weight of the numbers pressing against them. And some had started to climb up the walls, heading for the windows higher up. Glass that definitely wasn't protected by metallic mesh. They'd be inside here before too long.

Inside with me.

There was a back way out, through the mall itself. So I gave up on my plan of trying to reason with these people – could I still call them that? – and ran off, only to find the same was happening there was well. I didn't need to check the monitors to know that they had the mall surrounded, and I didn't need to ask them to know it wasn't Blu-rays, fashion accessories or sporting goods they were after. They wanted me, could smell me or something. Fresh meat – the only kind around here at the moment, it appeared. I was trapped, and still I could hear more of them arriving outside, more clamour, more rattling of bars, more glass cracking and smashing.

Then I remembered it. The grand draw! I'd even entered it myself, with the promise of perhaps winning the star prize. I raced up one lane, down another, until I came to the section of the mall I needed. And there it was, facing me. The most beautiful thing I've ever seen. A top of the range, brand new Land Rover, gleaming silver on its turntable stand – idle for the evening – encircled by red roping that looped onto brass stands. Worth about thirty odd grand, it wasn't its monetary value I was interested in, or grateful for, right at that moment. It was its sturdiness, its ability to knock most things out of its way. Thanking my lucky stars they hadn't been giving away something like a sports car, I just prayed the damned thing had fuel in its tank.

It was open, so I climbed in. There looked to be a full tank, but that wasn't the problem. Where the hell were the damned keys? I checked the glove compartment, under the sun visor. I was sitting in my means of escape, but had no way of getting the thing moving.

I slammed the steering wheel, just as I saw the first of the people, the – yes, say it, I told myself, unable to fight the evidence of my own eyes anymore – *dead* people rounding the corner of that section. They'd obviously broken down the mall's rear defences, and now I was stuck inside an even smaller space. I looked left and right. Then I spotted it, the booth where the people giving away the car always stood, where they sold their tickets. The keys had to be in there!

I didn't think twice about it, didn't even contemplate the idea that they might not be inside. I just opened the door again, leapt out, and covered the metres between the 4x4 and the booth in seconds. I took hold of the door handle and pulled. It was locked... *of course* it was locked. But I didn't have time to look for yet another set of keys. A quick glance over my shoulder told me I had very little time left at all, the deceased things stalking me were speeding up now they saw I was free of the vehicle.

My baton was out in seconds, smashing the glass window of the booth. No niceties now, no fear of repercussions – they could bill me later – just sheer desperation, and survival instinct.

I stuck my hand through, careful of the ragged edges; unlike those behind me, I wasn't immune to the pain of pierced skin. I reached around inside, conscious of the fact the group heading my way was growing in number, that they were still speeding up.

There! I found them, right on the table amongst clipboards and rolls of tickets. Grinning like an idiot, I snatched them up and turned. I wasn't out of the woods yet, not by a long chalk. In fact some of those dead people were so close I could practically feel their breath on me, if they'd had any breath to feel that was.

I had to swing the baton, clipping one fat guy in a cardigan to move him out of the way – there was just the slightest twinge of "what are you *doing*?", but then the man was missing part of his cheek already, a gaping hole allowing me to see through to the gum, teeth and tongue. Besides, they hadn't seemed to feel anything back at the entrance, had they? So it followed they wouldn't feel the wood of my day-stick as it smacked them up the side of the head. I cleared bodies out of the way like that: a bloated woman wearing a flowery dress; a young lad wearing only his boxer shorts; a lanky woman who looked to be in her 30s, or had been when she'd met her end, because her hair was falling out in clumps, eyeballs rolled back as if she was blind. I did that until the baton was snatched out of my hand...

But I finally made it to the Land Rover, climbing in and locking the door – though not without slamming one bony arm in it, tearing it off at the elbow. I jammed the key in the ignition and turned, offering up another silent thanks that she started first time. Then I clicked off the handbrake, stamping on the accelerator virtually at the same time. The vehicle lurched forward, not the smoothest of starts I have to say (actually, the worst since I had my first driving lesson, kangarooing it down our street). And suddenly there were body parts everywhere, clambering all over the Land Rover, climbing up and onto the roof, clinging to the back, like monkeys in a safari park. And just as dangerous.

I drove through the ones in front, barely seeing faces. Then she was in front of me, the little girl, couldn't have been more than five or six. Instinct kicked in and I braked, hard, lurching forward in the driver's seat. Ironically, it was this action that threw off the others that had been on my vehicle. When I looked up again, the girl was snarling, leaping forward onto the bonnet, drawing back a fist and punching the windscreen. *That's what you get*, I thought to myself, as I set off again, swinging the Land Rover to the side as much as I could – knocking those standing in front out of the way and shaking the girl off at the same time. There was a bump as she went under my back wheel, but as I looked in the rear view mirror, I saw her get up again, her body twisted round so that her legs faced one way and her torso and head the other.

I was still asleep, I had to be. Back in that office upstairs, dreaming that I was in some cheesy Friday night horror flick. Any second now I'd wake up, see that the monitors were clear and...

Something grabbed at my crotch, clamped on hard through my trousers. I let out a wail, losing concentration and veering off sideways momentarily to plough into a bookshop window display. I looked down, saw the bony hand there, what was left of the arm dangling from it.

How? How could that thing still be moving after I'd torn it from whatever creature it had belonged to? It just was, that's all I needed to know. And it gave me my first insight into just how hard those fuckers were to kill. No, not kill. How can you kill something that's already died? Incapacitate then. It was like every part of them could operate independently, even when detached from the rest. But I wasn't thinking about that, surprisingly. I was thinking about the fingers curled up and crushing my balls. I reached down with the hand not currently occupied with steering, and prised those fingers off – snapping them where I had to. Once the grip was loosened, I flung the whole thing over onto the passenger seat, but it just kept on coming, broken fingers and all. In the end I had to click the electric window down and toss the arm out, urging the glass up again as quickly as I could.

Those fingers that were still functional hooked over the rising window until it hit the top and sliced them off. I looked on in disgust as the chopped up tips wriggled down the inside of the glass, surfing a waterfall of goo. Moving in the same way those worms had done over those 'living' corpses at the entrance.

But I had bigger fish to fry, as I could see when I turned the corner to head for the entrance again. That section was completely filled with the dead; I mean no space at all to get through. The entrance itself was a complete mess of broken barriers and glass, where they'd forced their way in.

I wasn't sure if even the Land Rover could take it, but ultimately I had no choice. I pressed my foot down on the accelerator and ploughed on through. It was like driving in a sea of bodies, and it wasn't long before they began to slow me down through sheer weight of numbers. They battered the sides of the vehicle, just like they had with the mall's entrance, and I realised it wouldn't hold them out for long. Gritting my teeth, I kept stamping on the accelerator, coaxing more power, more speed out of it. I *had* to break through this wall of rotting flesh. Surely there couldn't be that many of the things?

Just when I thought it wouldn't end, the 4x4 pushed its nose through the last line of them, actually thickest towards the back. Then I felt it speed up, too fast in fact, out through the shattered entrance and forwards into a wall on the far side of the car park. The airbag promptly deployed, a good job as I hadn't put my seatbelt on, and I smacked into it.

Come on, get up. Carl, you have to get up and get out of there, right now! Move it soldier!

That voice I was hearing was my father's. I have no idea whether he actually sounded like that, I was too young to remember, but in times of stress I always hear it. And it always gets me moving. I needed to though, because, after shaking my head to clear it and looking behind me, I saw that the crowds of walking corpses had shifted their attention. After spending so long trying to get in, they were now rushing to follow me out.

I freed myself from the inflatable balloon, opening the door at the same time. I practically fell from the Land Rover onto the concrete below. But then I was up and running. I ran so fast, faster than I ever have in my life, grateful for the fact I try to keep myself in shape, that I go for all those jogs, even though my bum knee complains.

It started to do the same when I was about half a mile or so away from the mall, and only then did I stop and turn, looking back at the place from a distance. The dead that were there hadn't followed me – I guess jogging isn't their style – but they hadn't stuck around at the shopping precinct either. They were on the prowl again for meat, and now that I was gone, there was no point hanging out there, I guess.

Sand's place is only a bus ride from the mall (the reason I had to take the bus is the same reason I was at Sandra's in the first place, that fucking cow of an ex-wife of mine... now you know why I wanted that Land Rover so badly; and I got it, didn't I, after a fashion), and I made my way cautiously there – avoiding anyone and everyone. I couldn't be sure who was normal and who was...

Sand's place was on an estate just outside of town, which looked relatively quiet. I figured –

hoped – whatever had happened might have passed her by. But it was only quiet because it had hit the area and moved on. Everywhere I looked, houses had been broken into, windows smashed same as the mall, doors battered down. It got me moving towards Sandra's that bit quicker, I can tell you. But I really wish to God I'd stayed away.

Because when I got there, I found the door to her block had been ripped off its hinges, the corridor that led to the lifts and the stairs completely trashed. It looked pretty deserted though, so as long as Sandra had had the savvy to hide while the place was being attacked... What was I talking about? Those goons back at the mall hadn't left it alone till they knew for definite I was gone. Better that she'd gotten out, same as I did. Escaped, run off somewhere. But then how would *I* find her?

It didn't make much difference anyway, as it turned out. Not when I got to her flat on the third level, not when I saw how much blood there was leading up to the front door. No, not leading, trailing *away* from it. Like someone had been dragged from the place – kicking and screaming? Definitely not, judging from the inside of the flat. It looked as if someone had been stabbed in there, blood everywhere: smeared all over the walls, soaked into the carpet she'd only just bought. My little sister... This was just too much.

Tears welled in my eyes as I stared at the scene of devastation. All my life I've tried to protect her, look after her, keep her safe, just like Dad would have done if he'd been around. That was one of the other reasons why she let me stay, to pay me back a bit, I think. But I'd failed her when she needed me the most. Useless, fucking useless.

I was in such a state, I didn't realise anyone was behind me until it was too late. Until they were grabbing at me. I pulled away, and heard a ripping sound as a piece of my shirt came off in the thing's hand. Whirling, I took it in: a bloke in his 50s with salt and pepper hair and a beard; he was dressed in pyjamas and didn't look that bad, so maybe recently deceased? Died in the night, only to be brought back – perhaps in the last few minutes, seeing as he was on his own? Brought back as...

It didn't matter who'd he'd been, it was what he was now that counted. And what he represented: the bastards that had done for my sister. He made a noise that was a cross between a growl and a moan. I growled back, snarled like a dog in my anger. Then it was me doing the attacking, leaping towards him. I pushed him back, punching him in the face. There was no surprise from him at this, no wincing at the blows. He couldn't feel a fucking thing, but I carried on, pounding away. Then I pushed him back through the door to the stairs, shoving him down them. He tumbled over and over, smacking into the wall at the first bend, where he collapsed in a heap and lay still. I thought for a moment I'd made a mistake. Maybe he hadn't been dead at all? Maybe I'd mistaken a living person for one of *them*, and in my rage actually killed him?

When the man started to move, started to make that God-awful noise again, I knew there had been no mistake. He was attempting to pick himself up once more, as if nothing had happened – like a cartoon character who's just fallen from a cliff. Trying to stand on what were clearly broken legs, like it didn't matter. I couldn't have that. It was then I noticed the fire axe on the wall – something you see every day, but never really take notice of. 'In case of emergency, break glass' it said. Well this definitely qualified. I smashed the glass with my elbow, grabbed the axe and followed him down the stairs.

When I reached pyjama man, I really went to town on him – starting with removing those legs, so he'd never walk on them again. When I was finished, he was in quivering pieces, which I gaped at for quite some time.

Then I carried on down to the ground floor, wandered back out through the entrance, and into the night...

~

By the time dawn was breaking on New Year's Day, this new dawn of the dead, I'd wandered all the way into town.

I could hear the chaos from quite some way away, though – it was hard not to. If they'd gravitated anywhere after finishing up with the outskirts, it was into the cities, where the population was denser. More meat, more prey. The police and army were still trying to contain things, attempting to combat the threat, but they'd lost before they even began.

I quickly stumbled on one of the skirmishes,

where tanks and jeeps were being overrun. Machine guns and rockets were no use against their enemies, couldn't they see that? Obviously not, because they were pushing on with the fight instead of falling back and regrouping. I just couldn't help myself, watching all that slaughter. "Order the retreat!" I called from the sidelines, cupping a hand to my mouth in an effort to be heard from my position.

A helicopter circled overheard, some guy hanging from its open door. He had a sniper's rifle, and although his hits were accurate they did nothing to stop those on the receiving end. It was then that I saw one of the others, one of the creatures made from... what, dust, ash? Someone who'd been cremated, anyway, now walking around after forming itself back into some kind of figure. It broke off from the pack, heading towards a jeep that was approaching. It stood in front of the vehicle, allowed itself to be smashed into and destroyed. I frowned; why would it do that? Perhaps there was some part of it that recognised what it was and wanted out? *Was* there even a way out for their kind?

But I soon saw its true intention. The jeep swerved, suddenly out of control, before slamming into the side of a bank and overturning. One of the soldiers managed to crawl from the wreck, and it was at this point the ash-figure re-formed again, streaming out of the hood of the jeep, attacking the felled infantryman before he could get any further. It had actually allowed itself to be run into, so it could gum up the workings of that jeep!

The helicopter swooped in then, moving closer to the action – whipping up the wind and causing the dust-creature to draw back, away from the soldier. Too late, I spotted another one of the dead people on the top of a nearby office building. Seconds later, they'd flung themselves off it, and were dropping down onto the chopper. The blades made mincemeat of the corpse, splattering it everywhere, but this also threw the helicopter off balance, driving it down so that it couldn't pull up again. It crashed into a street-lamp, before upending and hitting the main road. Even though I was some distance away, I had to put my hand up to shield my face from the resultant explosion.

When I looked again, I saw those body parts the helicopter had spread everywhere, still moving, still doing their best to attack what soldiers and police were left on the "battlefield". It wasn't until later, when I had time to stop and think about it, that I realised this showed they were thinking. Not only that, they apparently had a plan, no matter how rudimentary. A strategy to beat us... at least in the here and now.

"Retreat!" I shouted again. "For the love of God, retreat..." They were getting creamed out there, and nobody seemed to be in charge at all. First rule of warfare, knowing when to fight and when not to. No doubt they were still following the orders of some government official somewhere who didn't know what the fuck they were doing. "Fall back!" Either they couldn't hear me or just weren't taking any notice, because they continued on. I was about to leave them all to it, when I spotted something: a handful of police officers, pinned down and encircled by the dead, their shotgun blasts doing little but knocking the walking corpses back a bit.

One of them was a young, female officer – she looked scared out of her wits.

She looked like Sandra.

I couldn't just leave her – them – to it. I hadn't been able to save my little sister, but maybe... *What are you waiting for, soldier?* came that voice of Dad's in my head again. My grip on the axe I was still holding tightened.

Without really thinking about it, I began moving forwards, heading closer to the action. The only way to get through an enemy like this was to chop them out of your path, not let them close in on you. I'd figured that out from my experiences already. So that's what I did – waded into the circle they'd created, swinging left and right, hamstringing where I could, decapitating and lopping off arms. Generally trying to provide an exit for those trapped officers. To be honest a lot of it was a blur, and if I thought I'd taken things out on that pyjama guy back at Sand's, then I hadn't seen anything yet. If I'd been thinking clearly, I wouldn't even have considered doing something so crazy. But somehow, I managed to get two of the cops out of there, including the female one. The others were gonners before I even reached them, dragged off and torn apart for food.

"Holy Christ! Thanks, mate," said the male officer, as I lead them away from the fracas – the dead just starting to realise what had happened, working out whether or not to come after us. "What now?"

"Now we get the fuck out of here," I told him, breaking into a run again.

~

We made for the outskirts of the city, hid in the woods to get our breath back.

When we stopped, the man introduced himself as Sergeant Tony Harris. "And that's WPC Alice O'Brien."

"Carl Maxwell," I said, shaking his hand. I held it out for Alice, but the young police woman still looked shell-shocked... understandably so. Her eyes were wide as she tried to get her head round all this.

They were supposed to be on crowd control overnight, Tony told me, but when it became clear all hell had broken loose, they'd been issued with guns and told to head into the thick of it. "To find and protect anyone still... you know, *all right*."

"You mean still alive?" I said. "As opposed to walking around without a pulse."

He nodded. "When the army moved in, we thought things would get better. But instead..." Tony asked me my story, so I'd told him the edited "highlights", without going into too much detail about my sister. When I'd finished, he said, "What do you think caused all this?"

It was a fair enough question, and one that hadn't even crossed my mind until now. I hadn't had time to stop and think about it, not with what had happened at the mall, with Sandra. And I realised that not only did I not have a clue, I also didn't give much of a shit. It had happened, and now those who were left had to deal with it.

And by deal, I meant fight back.

"But it's... You saw what was happening back there, what they could do. I lost a lot of colleagues... *friends* today. And if you hadn't come along..." Tony let the sentence trail off. "How are we supposed to fight something like *that*?"

"By being smart about things," I replied. "By picking our fights. By having a plan." It was something I'd learnt from them. "This war's only just starting, but if we talk like that then we've already lost."

Tony shook his head and I wasn't sure whether he was disagreeing with me, or just plain disillusioned. I wouldn't have blamed him if he was. Like the rest of us, his whole world had been turned upside down. And the most action he probably saw on a day-to-day basis was a rumble on the streets after last orders. But still, who was I to be arguing with him? A security man at Crescent View... sorry, ex-security man. And I was asking him to go back out there and fight these things, what, because of my sister? He'd lost more people than that today, and I didn't even know about his personal life, whether he might have a wife, kids out there somewhere. Whether he'd been able to check on them.

In the end it really didn't matter, because Tony was dead by the next day. And by dead, I mean one of *them*. He must have been bitten or scratched or something during the skirmish, because he turned overnight, while we were trying to get some rest. Went crazy, starting making those strange noises and just went for us. Quiet Alice – who'd been so stunned after I got her out – blew his head off with a shotgun at close range, just as Tony was about to bite *me*. I took over then with my axe...

She never spoke much about it afterwards, not even as we were burying the still trembling flesh I'd cut up – in separate spots, keeping it all apart – but I think they were close, those two. I think maybe he'd been her mentor or something when she first joined the force. Perhaps doing what she'd had to do fired her up enough to come round to my way of thinking, though.

"What you were saying earlier," she offered eventually. "About fighting back and all that?"

I nodded.

"Well, I'm in." She held her hand out this time, and I shook it. "There's nothing left for me here." And that was that, the start of it. The start of *everything*. I think we kept each other going through the next few weeks, next few months. Not in *that* way, there was never anything between Alice and me like that – more that we relied on each other. Knew we had one another's backs. She became my trusted second-in-command in the army we'd build up together. Without her, I'd never have made it through that final battle. Would never have made it to the end...

I'm skipping ahead again, aren't I? And you need to know about my band of soldiers; it's important stuff. Okay, so like all armies we started off small, but we were lucky. As we travelled from place to place, always moving, always trying to stay ahead of the dead things, scavenging for food and hiding out at night away from the population centres, we picked people up along the way. People who felt the same way we did, or came to think it once they'd encountered us.

The first of them was "the butcher". We didn't call him that because of the way he went at the dead, although we might as well have. No, Walker – he never told us whether this was his first or last name, and we never asked – had been an *actual* butcher before New Year's. He looked overweight, but had a speed that didn't tally with his size. Bald, with tattoos along the length of his arms, he looked more like a thug than someone you'd find on your local high street selling meat. We ran into him while we were making a run for supplies at the coast, and got cornered by a mob of Stiffs – which is what Alice and me decided to call them (we've never used the "Z" word; just didn't feel right, if you know what I mean?) – who took us by surprise. We ran down a dead end, they were advancing on us. Walker happened to be nearby, heard all the racket, and came to help us out. Cleavers were his weapon of choice, not surprisingly, and he certainly knew how to use them. Like us, he'd figured out the best way to dispatch Stiffs was divide and conquer, as in dividing them up. For those with a little less in the flesh department, he used a small chainsaw that dangled from his hip, which cut through bone like a warm knife through butter.

Once the fight was over, we got the story of what had happened to him. How he'd been driving through the night, on his way to a slaughterhouse out in the country for an early pick-up, and when he'd got there found the cuts of hanging meat jerking around on their hooks. "And I thought, that's funny," said Walker, rubbing his chin. Always the king of understatement. It was only when a cow that had just been killed with a bolt-gun got up again and bit one of the slaughterhouse workers, that Walker got it. When the inhabitants of a nearby cemetery came banging on the doors to get in, it just drove home what was happening. "I mean, I got out of there, though not without a scrap," Walker told us. "By the time I got home, back to the shop..." He bowed his head – he didn't need to tell us anymore. Walker had been on his own ever since, he said. "To be honest, I've preferred it that way. Only myself to look out for."

"You never heard of safety in numbers, Walker?" I asked.

"Didn't help her lot very much, did it?" he replied, nodding at Alice. I had to admit, he had me there. The police, and every other fucking defensive force we had... all pretty much useless against this new enemy.

"We're going to do things a bit differently," Alice said to him. "Hit them where it hurts."

"Yeah, you and whose army little lady?"

"Me and mine," I said to him, which sounded a lot better in my head than it did out loud. Walker laughed, and I couldn't help but join in. Even Alice was smirking in an 'I can't believe you just said that' kind of way.

"Join us," I said when it'd died down a bit, and Walker looked at me sideways, one eye half closed.

"All right, you mad bastard. All right."

Now there were three of us, and we added two more to what would become our central command unit the following weekend: a biker called Jim Telford, who passed us on the road while we were driving to the next town (in a world like this one had become, it wasn't hard to find transportation – finding the right sort, now that was different, and I was sticking with 4x4s – start as you mean to go on); and an ex-farmer's wife called Cathy Gifford. She was the one who came up with our best weapon to date, but I'll tell you a bit more about that later on.

Like Walker, Jim had wanted to stay on his own initially – though unlike my butcher friend, Jim had been a loner pretty much all his life. "Drifter, I suppose you'd call me," he told us, scratching his black moustache. He looked as if he'd come right off the set of *Easy Rider* or something, but spoke with a clear-cut English accent. He'd actually been born James Telford III, he explained when we knew him a bit better, and had managed to twist his arm into joining our rapidly expanding collection of resistance fighters (yes, I was starting to think along those lines: the Stiffs as an invading and occupying force, with us against them, trying to either drive them out or destroy them).

"A nob?" Walker had replied to that one.

"Not as much as you are," Jim had said, then smiled. Those two always did like to tease each other. Crucially, Jim had spent time in the services when he was younger; his family had insisted. "I got out as soon as I could, however," he said, which I never understood, being someone they wouldn't even consider. But it meant he had *some* military knowledge, and that would come in handy.

It was something our final recruit to the cause had in spades, too. We first came across Quinn when we spotted his plane in the sky, leaving a black streak of smoke in its wake as it was dragged back down to earth again. We followed it to a field over the horizon, where the plane had landed – well, *crashed* to be honest. And there he was, a lone, silver-haired figure crawling out of the wreckage. We knew he couldn't have been one of them, because they didn't drive or fly – at least we hadn't seen them do that. They just didn't seem interested; perhaps that stuff represented the old, human way of life.

So we approached him, but we didn't get very far. Either he'd been faking how severe his injuries were, or the man had such great reserves to draw on he put us all to shame. Either way, he was up and bounding towards Walker and Jim, taking them down in seconds. Knocking them unconscious with a couple of blows.

Gritting my teeth, I came at him next, but he avoided my clumsy attacks just as easily. In seconds, I was on the floor as well, a boot on my neck, arm backwards and being held by the pilot of the crashed plane. Alice and Cathy were approaching, but I held up a shaky hand to stop them.

"L-Listen," I managed, though it wasn't easy with the pressure on my throat, the pain in my shoulder. "W-We're not your enemy."

All I got was a grunt in reply.

"B-But... but I'm guessing you've seen enough to know who is." I had no idea at the time, the things Quinn had really seen.

Another grunt.

"We're... we're trying to fight back. Help us." I was hoarse by this point, on the verge of blacking out myself. Something in my voice must have registered with him, though, because he let go of me. I scrambled backwards, out of his reach – I later realised that he could have reached me easily, no matter how far away I was. Quinn was fast, faster than anyone I'd ever seen. I offered a croaky thanks to him, staring up at the silver-haired individual who had steely eyes to match. Not the best of first encounters, and I had no idea how I was going to convince him to join us – but I did know that we needed him.

Then Quinn said, in an accent that had just a trace of American in it, "What's your name, soldier?"

I couldn't help but smile at that one. It was the first time anyone – anyone *real* – had called me that, before or after the chaos. "M-Maxwell," I replied.

I was under no illusions about what would happen next, about the superiority, the seniority of this man – about how he'd take over. But that wasn't how it panned out at all. "I'm Quinn," he said, walking over to me slowly, grabbing my arm again, but helping me up this time. "And I'm ready when you are," he finished, going off to help up the other men he'd felled.

He never did tell us what he'd been before New Year's Day, but I was guessing some kind of covert operative, maybe even some sort of government assassin? But he did hint at things every now and again, offer us titbits about what state the rest of the world was in, enough to tell us that things weren't going that well *anywhere*. In many cases, seeing how the wind was blowing, they'd done what our government obviously hadn't had chance to. They'd used the ultimate weapon, Quinn told us, but all this had accomplished was killing off the survivors, leaving a wasteland behind. Not even bombs could get rid of those who weren't alive in the first place, who could come back together as ash – nuclear or otherwise. That was why he'd escaped over here, and why he'd hooked up with us, because I had the terrible feeling that we might be the only chance mankind had left.

Quinn moved like a cat and was just as unpredictable. He didn't take command of our unit (at times it didn't even feel like he was a part of it) but he did offer me advice where necessary, usually with a tip or shake of the head – he was a man of few words, Quinn – and I suppose I started to rely on that. I also thanked my lucky stars that we came across him, because that was the moment we really turned into an effective fighting force.

One finally to be reckoned with.

There were more members, of course – gangs that we found fighting their own private wars, which we absorbed into ours; pockets of resistance who were just waiting for us to come along, offer them some kind of direction – but that was the core group. Alice, Walker, Cathy, Jim, Quinn and me, as their leader. If I stopped to think about it too much, it made me feel physically sick, that responsibility. But it also made me feel useful for the first time ever in my life. And hopefully made Dad feel proud, wherever he was. Besides, I wasn't just doing this for our species, I was doing this for Sand. I'd make them pay, all right.

Our first major victory was the battle of Bedfield Avenue, though we'd had more than a few set-backs leading up to it (but we definitely learned from our mistakes). Our scouts came upon a kind of "community" of Stiffs, the chance to take out quite a number in one go all in one place. We couldn't let that pass. So, we hit them when they were least expecting it, and head on.

First we fired flare guns into the crowd, setting fire to some of the Stiffs, blinding others; we'd discovered that, yes, you can still damage the retinas of these things. Then, in the confusion, Jim and Alice moved in, both on motorbikes – he'd been giving her some pointers on one of those. They spread out a net of barbed wire between them, encircled the dead and tangling them up in it.

Walker moved in next, chopping them to pieces – it was as easy as shooting fish in a barrel. Those that were turning to ash, because of the flares, or were ash already and attempting to damage the vehicles we were using, were in for a big shock. I'd gotten the idea when the helicopter had blown that ash thing back during that first fight I'd encountered. All it had taken was some portable generators and fans large enough and they didn't stand a chance. They might be able to come back, re-form, but they sure as shit couldn't get close enough to do anything when we turned those on them. Plus we'd sealed up all possible gaps on our trucks and cars, so they wouldn't be able to gum up the works so easily.

Quinn walked amongst them like he didn't give a fuck, doing more damage with his hands than the rest of my men – that's how I starting to think about them, as *my* men – could do with all their weapons combined. Blink and you'd miss it, but he took off heads, snapped arms and legs in half, piled up the Stiffs and made sure they weren't in a fit shape to do any damage. That was the key, you see – incapacitate, then deal with the disposal later on.

And while we disposed of some straight away, we interrogated others. Not that we got anything out of them.

"It's just noise," Jim would say, listening in on our questioning. But I knew better, and so did Quinn. I'd seen them "talking" to each other, communicating. It was how they'd formed their battle plans. We'd crack it at some point, especially as we'd recruited a few brain-boxes to our burgeoning militia.

There were celebrations that night after the battle, but I didn't join in. Didn't see any cause for rejoicing in the long run. We'd taken down a few Stiffs, so what? There were always more where they came from.

I stood, leaning on a tree and watching the dancing figures round the fire, those that weren't on watch. Some handing round bottles, others hooking up – I spotted Cathy and Walker heading off, hand in hand. I almost stopped them, but Alice put a hand on my arm and shook her head. "Let them blow off steam while they can. This is going to be a long haul, but we've drawn our first blood." A strange phrase seeing as the Stiffs don't bleed; well, not in any kind of way we were used to. But she was right, of course. You had to cut people slack sometimes, it meant you'd get more out of them. And it meant you'd always have their loyalty.

Alice was also right that this would be a long and drawn out affair, but after that first victory, more of those followed than defeats. It was as if with every one, we were building up to something. Chipping away at the Stiffs little by little.

I said earlier that Cathy came up with probably our best weapon, didn't I? So I suppose I'd better put you out of your misery and tell you what it was. Nothing hi-tech, no bells and whistles or anything, it was simply a piece of machinery that the workers had once used on her farm. We'd tested it out on a handful of Stiffs at first, luring them into a spot where we could fire it up.

Leading them right into the spinning blades of a combine harvester, ripping those Stiffs to bits in seconds, not leaving enough of them to put up a fight – although we'd bury the individual pieces separately, as I'd learned to do right from the start. "Chew on that," she'd call down as she mowed into them, grinning.

It was how she'd come across the one who

looked like he might be leading them. The big bastard with a scar down his cheek... But we'll get to him in a bit.

Later we'd use it in full scale conflicts, because it could decimate their numbers in no time. We'd eventually refer to the collection of these we gathered as our heavy artillery. There was no point thinking about war like we used to, fighting with bombs and bullets (we'd all seen where that had got our regular armed forces). We needed to be smarter about our tactics, rely more on ideas like this. It was one of the reasons why I initiated a regular brain-storming session, which lead to other weapons such as water cannons – put forward by an ex-fireman in our ranks called Gerry Sessions – and the notion of trapping the dead in spaces where we could lower the temperature dramatically and suddenly, freezing them in more ways than one. It was easy then to just snap bits off and get rid of them in the usual way.

It never occurred to me that what we might be doing was actually *in*-human, that it might seem to them like atrocities, the same way we used to look back on the kinds of acts Hussein or Gaddafi were responsible for in the time before.

Or maybe it did and I pushed those thoughts down. If they could "talk" to each other in those grunts of theirs, why not be able to form attachments, why not be able to... to feel? After all, there are other ways of experiencing pain, aren't there?

Speaking of which, that was how the whole final conflict came about. We'd been intercepting strange radio messages for a while – and though we dismissed them at first as just noise, even an idiot could tell after listening for a bit that it was the moans and groans of those Stiffs out there. Maybe the idea of them using radios to communicate seemed so out of whack with who, or what, they were that we dismissed it as nonsense, or impossible. But for me it only strengthened the argument that they were thinking, that they were reasoning.

How we eventually translated them was another matter. It was Quinn's suggestion, using volunteers or people who'd been bitten or scratched already to bridge the gap. People who were freshly infected were the best, as they held out the longest, remained human for the greatest length of time. But they were the hardest to watch. Walker would take a Stiff's head, holding it by the hair, and bring it closer to "the subject" as Quinn would call them. I had a sneaking suspicion it wasn't the first time he'd done stuff like this, in similar dark rooms, locked away from the eyes of the world. But man, those snapping teeth, coming closer and closer to arms or legs. Then, once the bite had happened, it would usually take anything from half an hour to a couple of hours before the subject would be able to take those gurgles coming over the airwaves and turn them into English – we'd have someone sitting close by with a notepad, ready to jot everything down. It would then take anything from three to nine hours for our subject to fully turn.

I was present every single time.

I don't think I'll ever forget the way it would start to come on. The twitching, the slurring of words, sounding like a drunken person, to match those strange movements: the reason I'd mistaken them for pissheads back at the mall that first time round. If the subjects hadn't been strapped down they would have been up and at us, lunging towards us. As it was it still looked very disturbing. Reminded me of when Grampa got dementia: it was him but not him. It still looked like the person you knew, but they were different... *strange*. And sometimes, before the turn came on, they'd talk half in Stiff language, half in ours.

"Grraahhh... can't win... hugghhhhonly chance is to... trrgghhh join them... urrghhhhussss..." Spittle would fly from their mouths, cords would strain on the neck. Walker and Quinn usually disposed of the "remains" before they could creep us out too much. It was worth it, though, for the intel.

We learnt that there had been a revolt of sorts amongst their ranks. That huge scarred Stiff Cathy had come across, sending his troops into battle, was gone. Replaced by someone with more savvy. Someone who was calling the brethren to arms – or at least that's how it appeared to us. He was drawing the other Stiffs to a homebase, at any rate, the location of which we learned from those transmissions. And, appropriately enough, it was a graveyard. A heavily fortified and protected graveyard, and crawling with their kind. More each and every day we had it under surveillance. During these reccies, we also identified their HQ at the heart of that cemetery – a kind of huge mausoleum – and their leader, a man who appropriately enough seemed to have his *own* female second-in-command.

The whole place was like some kind of Mecca for them. Somewhere we'd been looking for all this time. The perfect spot to hit if we wanted to make a statement, if we wanted to *really* hurt the Stiffs.

I didn't know whether taking it down would do anything in the long run, maybe I thought it would be like hitting the mothership in some crappy SF flick, which would, in turn, see all the drones falling like dominoes. The consensus amongst us all was certainly in favour. Quinn remained silent during the meeting, but then that was nothing new. The rest of my high command more than made up for it.

"I say we hit them, hit them fast – and we hit them hard!" said Walker.

"If we go in all guns blazing, we forfeit our element of surprise," Alice pointed out, and I'd never been prouder of her. She'd come a long way, learnt so much in the months since all this started.

"Fuck the element of surprise, I *want* them to see who's coming for them!" snapped our butcher.

"They'll smell you first," said Jim, and Walker flipped him the bird.

"I'm with Walker," said Cathy, which was no great surprise. "I've been training up squads to use the threshers. We have a pretty good line of attack there."

"Granted," I replied. "But I've always said the way to win this is by being smart about it. By not rushing in blindly. So how about this..." They listened as I outlined the plan, which I'd already run by Quinn, all of them nodding their agreement. So, with instructions given and a date set, we prepared ourselves for a concerted push against the Stiffs.

On the eve of that battle, I found Quinn alone and sipping whiskey on the roof of the office building we'd taken over as *our* base of operations. He was gazing out across the skyline as the sun went down on yet another day in this nightmarish world. He didn't acknowledge my presence, but his body language told me he knew I was there. And when he bent and offered me a glass without looking, that just confirmed it. I poured a generous amount of the liquid from the bottle into my tumbler, gulped it down, relishing its fire in my belly. I'd need even more of that fire before the next day was out.

I'd never been interested before, never really

cared, but I found myself saying: "You know what happened, don't you. Why all this came about." It wasn't a question. Something inside told me that he knew all right. I just felt it.

Quinn looked at me and answered simply, "We brought this on ourselves." It wasn't quite an answer, didn't tell me whether it was to do with some kind of experiment, or even some sort of Biblical thing, but at the same time it told me enough – and I never pushed him for any more. Never had the chance to.

I thought about asking then if he'd had any family. Perhaps I was angling for him to tell me I was like that son he'd lost or never had, or something equally crap and schmaltzy. I liked to imagine it panning out that way, even though it never really happened. But the moment was gone, along with the sun.

And then so was Quinn.

First thing the next morning, we set off. The date seemed appropriate: New Year's Day, exactly one year since all this had happened. We'd been fighting so long, had lost so much...

My plan was simple, and combined both lots of suggestions.

First, Quinn would lead a team in from the

rear, taking Walker with him. They'd penetrate the defences at their weakest point, then make sure the way would be clear for our main attack from the front: led by Cathy and her combines. At the same time, teams would be hitting the graveyard from the side – one led by Jim, one by Alice, both jumping the walls using motorbikes.

We'd be using every trick in our repertoire – new ideas like industrial strimmers for close-quarter combat, water pistols and rifles filled with acid – hitting them with everything we had.

And me? I was coming in from above, hang-gliding silently in to go straight for the jugular. That mausoleum and their leader within it, once everything had kicked off as a distraction. Yes, it went against everything every warfare or military expert had ever said. I should have been well away from it all, safe, while I sent the footsoldiers in to clear a path. But that had never been my style, to hide away while other people took those kinds of risks for me. Besides which, we weren't holding anything back. If this went wrong, then there would *be* no resistance left to lead. This was the battle that would prove the turning point in the entire war.

I watched the early stages through binoculars

from above, getting radio reports back at every stage – on a different frequency to the one *they* used, of course. And it seemed to go like a dream. Quinn and his squad infiltrated the graveyard with no problems at all, in fact the whole place seemed pretty much deserted.

What defences they had at the gate – that included an annoying, but easily subdued yapping dog, which we nailed with a net-gun – were swept aside, making way for our guys. Alice and Jim stormed the sides, looking like something out of *The Great Escape*, only they were breaking in, not out. All efforts to combat and repel us were failing. I remember grinning as I angled the glider, smug bastard that I was.

It was only as I came in to land that everything went tits up. That it all turned on a penny. I'd been smart, but there'd been someone here cleverer than me, who made me look like just some dumb grunt. Because the Stiffs had a few surprises of their own, and all they'd been doing was biding their time until they could spring their trap.

You see, somehow they'd known all along we were coming.

I was joined by Quinn and his team shortly

after I climbed out of the harness: the plan being to enter the mausoleum now and find their leader, plus his female right hand.

"Good work everyone," I called out, gripping my trusty axe, still my weapon of choice after all this time. Looking back, what a fucking idiot I was – playing at being a general or something, thinking I knew it all. "Now we can—"

And suddenly, they were there: they were *everywhere*. Rising from their hiding places in the earth, none of them needing air to breathe, taking our lot just as much by surprise as we'd hoped to with them. Swarming over Cathy's combines and getting into the cabs before the drivers could do a thing, switching off those deadly blades. Dragging Jim and Alice's bikes down into the ground like they were in the middle of an earthquake or something, front wheels up and spinning in the air.

And I only just managed to dodge the cleaver swing from Walker, my reflexes at their sharpest by now and fuelled by adrenalin. "What the f—" I said, ducking back and avoiding a second blow, but losing my grip on my axe at the same time. His face was glazed over, eyes not really seeing me.

Then I saw why... We'd blown those fucking ash-things away, patted ourselves on our backs as we dispersed them, scattering them. So instead of re-forming, they'd made a new home in Walker, were still streaming into his nose and ears, turning those glassy eyes black like coals in a snowman. Taking over the functions of his body, turning him against his comrades in arms.

All around, the same thing was happening: those fuckers going all Body Snatcher on us; at the same time decimating our numbers. Reducing the ranks of those still on our side, but also making sure we couldn't fight back because these were our friends for Christ's sake. People we knew and... yes, loved. Who still looked the same (not in the same way Stiffs did, though) apart from those damned black eyes.

I dodged another blow, ducking and kicking out Walker's legs from beneath him – bringing an elbow down hard on his stomach to wind him momentarily. I needed to gather my thoughts. I needed...

Quinn. I looked to him then, just like I always had since he'd come along. But just like he had on the roof the night before, he was gone again.

Didn't take long to spot him, however. He was making for the mausoleum, taking down Stiffs left and right as he did so. At least he was still okay, I thought to myself. And he was carrying on with the plan regardless, trying to cut the head off the snake.

Suddenly there *He* was, the leader. The mountain coming to Mohammed. He emerged from that stone place, girl by his side. Both rotting, scabby things to my eyes, he was walking oddly, as if both his legs had been mangled at some point. Perhaps they'd thought it safe to come out now, survey the scene of their victory. But there was still a chance to win the day, in spite of what was going on all around us, the crushing defeat that was still playing out – which I was still in denial about. If Quinn could just...

But he slowed as he reached them, looking back at me.

"Do it! What's wrong...? Take them down!" I cried. Then I was crying for another reason, Jim – his eyes black and grainy – had just embedded my own discarded axe in my knee. My good knee at that! I howled in pain, falling over sideways as he yanked it out again, twisting shattered bone at the same time. Now I knew what those Stiffs felt like on the receiving end of my blade.

Jim hefted the weapon again, swinging it over his head. He was about to bring it down on me, my raised hand no defence to it, when his riding partner – and my trusted second – Alice, dived in front of it, taking the blow in her shoulder and shoving Jim back at the same time. Her eyes were clear, yet narrow with pain, when she called back weakly:

"Go!"

"Alice..."

"Carl, get the fuck out of here!"

I gaped, open-mouthed, then I heard that voice again. The one I imagined my dad's had been like, the one I hadn't heard recently, replaced by Quinn's... who'd let me down when I needed him the most. Just like I'd done with Sandra.

It said: *You know what the first rule of warfare is, Carl. Do what she says, get out of there. Come on, move it soldier!*

And I knew then, this was just as much of a dead end as the one we'd hit when Walker rescued Alice and me. I stemmed the blood flow as best I could with a shaky hand, and crawled away, a virtual cripple. I scrambled off, leaving a trail of red behind me. I remember thinking, least I'm in the right place if it all ends now.

I crawled through all that devastation, for some reason the Stiffs leaving me alone. I thought maybe they were all just occupied, or perhaps I wasn't worth bothering about. This great human leader reduced to the level of a garden slug, leaving a trail of crimson slime in my wake.

Not even that dog bothered with me, free now and getting stuck into those soldiers not infected, turned or being eaten – because I saw now the disgusting sight of Stiffs munching down on flesh, tearing into guts with their teeth, chewing on legs, shoulders, feet.

I almost threw up, though that was probably more from the pain in my leg. I was seeing stars dancing in front of me. If it wasn't for that voice in my head, urging me on, then I'd probably have given up.

I made it out through those ruined gates, though, made it down the street where the cemetery was located before I blacked out the first time. Made it quite a way from the graveyard, passing out a couple more times, before I heard someone coming after me.

I looked over my shoulder, saw Quinn's face, swimming in my field of vision, just before I passed out for the final time.

Saw Quinn's face, but heard my dad's voice once more.

You've done well, son. You did your best...

I'm proud of you.

~

But that isn't where we end it. This story, *my* story, linked as it is to that of the human race and the race that followed it.

When I woke, I was surrounded by stone. I'd got my wish, found myself inside that mausoleum: the ultimate aim of my mission. And there, in front of me, was the Stiffs' leader and his female counterpart... who had children with her. Dead fucking children! They hid behind her, peeking out at this stranger in their midst.

I was on a chair, slumped forward, but not bound in any way. My wound had been bandaged, quite neatly. I couldn't feel any pain.

"His name is David. Hers is Helen, she's the one who fixed up your leg." A female voice, someone who appeared from behind me. "She knows first aid, used to be a teacher back in... well, back when she was alive."

"A... Alice?" I managed.

She was pretty messed up – my axe, wielded by Jim, having done some serious damage. But she was still alive... kind of. "We've been talking."

Now I knew, right there and then, that she wouldn't be a living thing for long. Alice could understand both species, which meant she'd been scratched or bitten. Infected. Either way, she didn't have much time; though maybe more than I had.

"They explained it all to me, and it makes sense. It actually makes perfect sense, Carl." She smiled. The fuckers had got to her, brainwashed her.

"Alice, how could you... They're—"

"They're *us*, Carl. That's all. Nothing to be frightened of. When you understand how all this works, you get what they're about." So she told me, and though I didn't like it – there were still Stiffs... sorry, the Risen (it's what David calls them; the other name is derogatory apparently), anyway there were still some of them that didn't actually like it either – I understood it.

Far from being individual pieces, they're all parts of a whole. The Risen, every single one of them, every single *bit* of them, they're all connected. Even the people who'd been eaten, all still part of it. A consciousness, when it's finished calibrating itself, that will be more powerful than anything in this world. Probably in the universe. The next step in our evolution, an undying mass.

A family, just like me and my soldiers had been. There was no choice, I'd become one of them whether I liked it or not, simply by dying right there in front of them from blood loss. The only choice I had was whether I wanted to speed things up, get infected just like Alice had been. The rest of my troops were either in the process of being bitten or already had been.

Alice turned back from David, who was making those strange moaning noises, and she nodded. "Right, I'll tell him... David says, think about it. No more injury, no more pain. His legs were broken in a car accident, but he can walk again now." That smile once more. "You'd be able to, as well."

The more Alice... the more the three of them talked, the more sense it seemed to make. Either that or I was going crazy. But I still railed against it, until they played their trump card, that is.

I said they were a family, but they'd also found mine.

David, Helen and the children stepped aside, and there was Sandra. Battered, bruised, caked in dried blood, but it was her. She smiled too, revealing several missing teeth. "She answered the call, just like the others," Alice explained.

I began to cry. No, I sobbed like a baby. My sister – here and alive. Well, here at any rate. I heard my father's voice again, repeating that first rule of warfare. And I knew it was time to stop fighting them.

"They want you to take command of their forces, Carl. Well, us really. There are still people out there like we were. Who need to see things more clearly."

I gave a nod. In fact, I nodded so hard my head hurt. When Alice began to turn, I let her... no, I *demanded* that she bite me. Turn me too. I wanted to be able to get up, to hug Sand.

So that's it, soon this whole thing will be over for me. I'll start a new life, on New Year's Day. Oh, wait a minute. There's one more thing you'll probably be wondering about. How did David know we were coming? That's an easy one to answer: they'd had intel of their own.

Information passed on to them from inside our own camp... from Quinn.

At one time I might have called him a traitor, but he didn't know what he was doing. Didn't even know he was giving things away. Wasn't through anything as crude as the ash people taking him over; it was more subtle than that. Minute samples from the Risen, injected into a captured human, allowing a degree of control over the speed of the turning. Slowing it to a crawl but at the same time ensuring a certain amount of influence over the subject – not that Quinn could remember the procedure (he'd been in a dark room all right, shut away from the world). Quinn had been *sent* to us, the ultimate sleeper agent. It was just a happy coincidence – for them – that he turned out to be such a replacement father figure for me. His secret reports were then translated by volunteers on their side, those bitten who could speak both languages, who were able to decipher what Quinn was telling them.

He's a clever bastard that David. Cleverer than I am, so I don't feel that bad about being outsmarted when all things are considered. He's even on the verge of coming up with food that'll sustain us, fake flesh which means all the Risen from now on can remain in one piece. Made me feel pretty guilty about what I did with those bits from the chopped up dead; separating them is the worst form of torture imaginable. First thing I'll do when I'm "well" again is try and fix some of that...

Now that really is it. They say all good things must come to an end. Some bad things, as well. Our existence as an inferior species, for example.

That's what's happening here, things are coming to a head – one way or another, things are ending. My old life. It's been a long, hard-fought battle, but at last, at long last there's a winner. And if you can't beat 'em...

My name is Carl Maxwell. I'm still alive, but not for much longer...

And that's when my new life will begin.

Also by Paul Kane:

Novels
Arrowhead (Abaddon, 2008)
Broken Arrow (Abaddon, 2009)
Arrowland (Abaddon, 2010)
Hooded Man (Omnibus) (Abaddon, 2013)
The Gemini Factor (Screaming Dreams, 2010)
Of Darkness and Light (Thunderstorm Books, 2010)
Lunar (Bad Moon Books, 2012)
Sleeper(s) (Crystal Lake Publishing, 2013)
The Rainbow Man (as P.B. Kane) (Rocket Ride Books, 2013)
Blood RED (SST Publications, 2015)
Sherlock Holmes and the Servants of Hell (Solaris Books, 2016)
Before (Grey Matter Press, 2017)
Deep RED (SST Publications, 2018)

Novellas & Novelettes
Signs of Life (Crystal Serenades, 2005)
The Lazarus Condition (Tasmaniac Publications, 2007)
Dalton Quayle Rides Out (Pendragon Press, 2007)
RED (Skullvines Press, 2008)

Pain Cages (Books of the Dead, 2011)
Creakers (chapbook) (Spectral Press, 2013)
The Curse of the Wolf (Hersham Horror Books, 2014)
Flaming Arrow (Abaddon, 2015)
The P.I.'s Tale (2016)
Snow (Stormblade Productions, 2016)
End of the End (Abaddon, 2016)
The Crimson Mystery (SST, 2016)
The Rot (Horrific Tales, 2016)
Beneath the Surface (with Simon Clark) (SST, 2017)

Collections
Alone (In the Dark) (BJM Press, 2001)
Touching the Flame (Rainfall Books, 2002)
FunnyBones (Creative Guy Publications, 2003)
Peripheral Visions (Creative Guy Publications, 2008)
The Adventures of Dalton Quayle (Mundania Press, 2011)
Shadow Writer (Mansion House Books, 2011)
The Butterfly Man and Other Stories (PS Publishing, 2011)
The Spaces Between (Dark Moon Books, 2013)
Ghosts (Spectral Press, 2013)
Monsters (Alchemy Press, 2015)

Shadow Casting (SST Publications, 2016)
Nailbiters (as Paul B Kane) (Black Shuck Books, 2017)
Death (The Sinister Horror Company, 2017)
Disexistence (Cycatrix Press, 2017)
The Life Cycle (Black Shuck Books, 2017)
Kane's Scary Tales: Volume 1 (Oz Horror Con, 2018)
Lost Souls (Shadowridge Press, 2018)

Non-Fiction
The Hellraiser Films And Their Legacy (McFarland)
Voices in the Dark (McFarland, 2010)
Shadow Writer – The Non-Fiction. Vol. 1: Reviews (BearManor Media)
Shadow Writer – The Non-Fiction. Vol. 2: Articles & Essays (BearManor Media)

Visit Paul Kane at his website:
shadow-writer.co.uk

*Now available and forthcoming from
Black Shuck Shadows:*

Shadows 1 – The Spirits of Christmas
                              by Paul Kane

Shadows 2 – Tales of New Mexico
                              by Joseph D'Lacey

Shadows 3 – Unquiet Waters
                              by Thana Niveau

Shadows 4 – The Life Cycle
                              by Paul Kane

Shadows 5 – The Death of Boys
                              by Gary Fry

Shadows 6 – Broken on the Inside
                              by Phil Sloman

Shadows 7 – The Martledge Variations
                              by Simon Kurt Unsworth

Shadows 8 – Singing Back the Dark
                              by Simon Bestwick

Shadows 9 – Winter Freits
　　　　　　　　by Andrew David Barker

Shadows 10 – The Dead
　　　　　　　　by Paul Kane

Shadows 11 – The Forest of Dead Children
　　　　　　　　by Andrew Hook

Shadows 12 – At Home in the Shadows
　　　　　　　　by Gary McMahon

blackshuckbooks.co.uk/shadows

Lightning Source UK Ltd.
Milton Keynes UK
UKHW021202150219
337360UK00005B/109/P

9 781913 038021